Linda Lael M
frontier her ov
more so than
series that b
share an inheritance—2,500 acres of
timber and high-country grassland
called Primrose Creek.

In this wonderful new series, four cousins discover
the dangers and the joys, the hardship and the
beauty, of frontier life. And each, in her own way,
finds a love that will last an eternity. Join the
McQuarry women in a special celebration of the
love, courage, and family ties that made the West
great.

Four special women. Four extraordinary stories.

THE WOMEN OF
PRIMROSE CREEK

BRIDGET

CHRISTY

SKYE

MEGAN

Praise for Linda Lael Miller's bestselling series

SPRINGWATER SEASONS

"A DELIGHTFUL AND DELICIOUS MINI-SERIES. . . . *Rachel* will charm you, enchant you, delight you, and quite simply hook you. . . . *Miranda* is a sensual marriage-of-convenience tale guaranteed to warm your heart all the way down to your toes. . . . The warmth that spreads through *Jessica* is captivating. . . . The gentle beauty of the tales and the delightful, warmhearted characters bring a slice of Americana straight onto readers' 'keeper' shelves. Linda Lael Miller's miniseries is a gift to treasure."

—*Romantic Times*

"This hopeful tale is . . . infused with the sensuality that Miller is known for."   —*Booklist*

"All the books in this collection have the Linda Lael Miller touch."   —*Affaire de Coeur*

"Nobody brings the folksiness of the Old West to life better than Linda Lael Miller."   —*BookPage*

"Another warm, tender story from the ever-so-talented pen of one of this genre's all-time favorites."

—*Rendezvous*

"Miller . . . create[s] a warm and cozy love story."
—*Publishers Weekly*

Books by Linda Lael Miller

Linda Lael Miller

The Women of Primrose Creek

Bridget

SONNET BOOKS

New York London Toronto Sydney Singapore

This book is a work of fiction. Names, characters, places and incidents are products of the author's imagination or are used fictitiously. Any resemblance to actual events or locales or persons, living or dead, is entirely coincidental.

An *Original* Publication of POCKET BOOKS

A Sonnet Book published by
POCKET BOOKS, a division of Simon & Schuster Inc.
1230 Avenue of the Americas, New York, NY 10020

Copyright © 2000 by Linda Lael Miller

ISBN: 0-671-04244-0

First Sonnet Books printing May 2000

10   9   8   7   6   5   4   3   2   1

SONNET BOOKS and colophon are trademarks of Simon & Schuster Inc.

Cover art by Robert Hunt

Printed in the U.S.A.

For Anita Carter,
the sweetest voice in any choir,
with love

Midsummer 1867

Primrose Creek, Nevada

Chapter

1

 race was on foot when she saw him again, carrying a saddle over one shoulder, a gloved hand grasping the horn. His hat was pushed to the back of his head, and his pale, sun-streaked hair caught the sunlight. His blue-green eyes flashed bright as sun on water, and the cocky grin she knew oh-so-well curved his mouth. Oh, yes. Even from the other side of Primrose Creek, Bridget knew right off who he was—trouble.

She had half a mind to go straight into the cabin for Granddaddy's shotgun and send him packing. Might have done it, too, if she hadn't known he was just out of range. The scoundrel had probably figured out what she was thinking, for she saw that lethal grin broaden for a moment, before he tried, without success, to look serious again. He knew he was safe, right enough, long as he kept his distance.

She folded her arms. "You just turn yourself

right around, Trace Qualtrough, and head back to wherever you came from," she called.

No effect. That was Trace for you, handsome as the devil himself and possessed of a hide like a field ox. Now, he just tipped the brim of that sorry-looking hat and set his saddle down on the stream bank, as easily as if it weighed nothing at all. Bridget, a young widow who'd spent three months on the trail from St. Louis, with no man along to attend to the heavier chores, knew better.

"Now, Bridge," he said, "that's no way to greet an old friend."

Somewhere inside this blatantly masculine man was the boy she had known and loved. The boy who had taught her to swim, climb trees, and ride like an Indian. The boy she'd laughed with and loved with an innocent ferocity that sometimes haunted her still, in the dark of night, after more than a decade.

Bridget stood her ground, though a fickle part of her wanted to splash through the creek and fling her arms around his neck in welcome, and hardened her resolve. This was not the Trace she remembered so fondly. This was the man who'd gotten her husband killed, sure as if he'd shot Mitch himself. "You just get! Right now."

He had the effrontery to laugh as he bent to hoist the saddle up off the ground. Bridget wondered what had happened to his horse even as she told herself it didn't matter to her. He could walk all the way back to Virginia as far as she cared, long as he left.

"I'm staying," he said, and started through the knee-deep, sun-splashed water toward her without even taking off his boots. "Naturally, I'd rather I was welcome, but your taking an uncharitable outlook on the matter won't change anything."

Bridget's heart thumped against the wall of her chest; she told herself it was pure fury driving her and paced the creek's edge to prove it so. "I declare you are as impossible as ever," she accused.

He laughed again. "Yes, ma'am." Up close, she saw that he'd aged since she'd seen him last, dressed in Yankee blue and riding off to war, with Mitch following right along. There were squint lines at the corners of his blue-green eyes, and his face was leaner, harder than before, but the impact of his personality was just as jarring. Bridget felt weakened by his presence, in a not unpleasant way, and that infuriated her.

Mitch, she thought, and swayed a little. Her bridegroom, her beloved, the father of her three-year-old son, Noah. Her lifelong friend—and Trace's. Mitch had traipsed off to war on Trace's heels, like a child dancing after a piper, certain of right and glory. And he'd died for that sweet, boyish naïveté of his.

"I've got nothing to say to you," Bridget said to him.

He took off his hat and swiped it once lightly against his thigh, in a gesture that might have been born of either annoyance or simple frustration, the distinction being too fine to determine. "Well," he replied, in a quiet voice that meant he was digging in to outstubborn her, should things come to that pass, "*I've* got plenty to say to *you,* Bridget McQuarry, and you're going to hear me out."

His gaze strayed over her shoulder to take in the cabin, such as it was. The roof of the small stone structure had fallen in long before Bridget and Skye, her younger sister, and little Noah had finally arrived at Primrose Creek just two months before, after wintering at Fort Grant, a cavalry installation at the base of the Sierras. Right away, Bridget had taken the tarp off the Conestoga and draped it over the center beam, but it made a wretched substitute. Rain caused it to droop precariously and often dripped through the worn cloth to plop on the bed and table and sizzle on the stove.

Trace let out a low whistle. "I didn't get here any too soon," he said.

Just then, Skye came bounding around the side of the cabin, an old basket in one hand, face alight with pleasure. She was sixteen, Skye was, and all the family Bridget had left, except for her son and a pair of snooty cousins who'd passed the war years in England. No doubt, Christy and Megan had been sipping tea, having themselves fitted for silken gowns, and playing lawn tennis, while Bridget and their granddaddy tried in vain to hold on to the farm in the face of challenges from Yankees and Rebels alike.

Good riddance, she thought. The last time she'd seen Christy, the two of them had fought in the dirt like a pair of cats; they'd been like oil and water the whole of their lives, Christy and Bridget, always tangling over something.

"Trace!" Skye whooped, her dark eyes shining.

He laughed, scooped her into his arms, and spun her around once. "Hello, monkey," he said, with a sort of fond gruffness in his voice, before planting a brotherly kiss on her forehead.

Bridget stood to one side, watching and feeling a little betrayed. She and Skye were as close as two sisters ever were, but if you looked for a resemblance, you'd never guess they were related. Just shy of twenty-one, Bridget was small, with fair hair and skin, and her eyes were an intense shade of violet, "Irish blue," Mitch had called them. She gave an appearance of china-doll fragility, most likely because of her diminutive size, but this was deceptive; she was as agile and wiry as a panther cub, and just about as delicate.

Skye, for her part, was tall, a late bloomer with long, gangly legs and arms. Her hair was a rich chestnut color, her wide-set eyes a deep and lively brown, her mouth full and womanly. She was awkward and somewhat dreamy, and though she was always eager to help, Bridget usually just went ahead and did most things herself. It was easier than explaining, demonstrating, and then redoing the whole task when Skye wasn't around.

"You'll stay, won't you?" Skye demanded, beaming up at Trace. "Please, say you'll stay!"

He didn't so much as glance in Bridget's direction, which, she assured herself impotently, was a good thing for *him*. "I'm not going anywhere."

Behind the cabin, in the makeshift corral Bridget had constructed from barrels and fallen branches, the new horse neighed. He was her one great hope of earning a living, that spectacular black and white paint. She'd swapped both oxen for him, barely a week before, when a half dozen Paiute braves had paid her an alarming visit. His name, rightfully enough, was Windfall, for she'd certainly gotten the best of the trade. Granddaddy would have been proud.

People would pay good money to have their mares bred to a magnificent horse like Windfall.

Her little mare, Sis, tethered in the grassy shade of a wild oak tree nearby, replied to the stallion's call with a companionable nicker.

A muscle pulsed in Trace's jaw. Even after all that time and trouble, flowing between them like a river, she could still read him plain as the *Territorial Enterprise*. If there were horses around, Trace was invariably drawn to them. He was known for his ability to train untrainable animals, to win their trust and even their affection. All of which made her wonder that much more how he'd come to be walking instead of riding.

"Where's the boy?" he asked. "I'd like to see him."

Bridget sighed. Maybe if he got a look at Noah, he'd leave. If there was any justice in the world, the child's likeness to his martyred father would be enough to shame even Trace into moving on. "He's inside, taking his nap," she said shortly, and gestured toward the cabin.

"What happened to your horse?" Skye wanted to know. Skye had many sterling traits, but minding her tongue wasn't among them.

"That's a long story," Trace answered. He was already on his way toward the open door of the cabin, and Skye hurried along beside him. "It ends badly, too." He paused at the threshold to kick off his wet boots.

"Tell me," Skye insisted. Her delight caused a bittersweet spill in Bridget's heart; the girl had been withdrawn and sorrowful ever since they'd buried Granddaddy and headed west to claim their share of the only thing he'd had left to bequeath: a twenty-five-hundred-acre tract of land in the high country of Nevada, sprawled along both sides of a stream called Primrose Creek. Too much loss. They had all seen too much loss, too much grief.

Trace stepped over the high threshold and into the tiny house, just as if he had the right to enter. The place was twelve by twelve, reason enough for him to move on, even if he'd been an invited guest. Which, of course, he wasn't. "He took off," he said. "Nothing but a knothead, that horse."

Bridget, following on their heels, didn't believe a word of it, but she wasn't about to stir up another argument by saying so. Trace would have known better than to take up with a stupid horse, though she wasn't so sure about his taste in women. He'd probably lost the animal in a game of some sort, for he was inclined to take reckless chances and always had been.

Noah, a shy but willful child, so like Mitch, with his wavy brown hair and mischievous hazel eyes, that it still struck Bridget like a blow whenever she looked at him, sat up in the middle of the big bedstead, rubbing his eyes with plump little fists and then peering at Trace in the dim, cool light.

"Papa," he said. "That's my papa."

A strained silence ensued. Bridget merely swallowed hard and looked away. She would have corrected her son, but she didn't trust herself to speak.

Trace crossed the small room and reached out for the boy, who scrambled readily into his arms. The little traitor.

"Well," Trace said, his voice thick with apparent emotion. "Hullo, there."

"He calls everybody 'Papa,' " Bridget blurted, and then, mortified, turned to the stove and busied herself with pots and kettles, so Trace wouldn't see her expression.

Trace chuckled and set his hat on the boy's head, covering him to the shoulders, and Noah's delighted giggle echoed from inside. "Does he, now?"

"Some of the folks in town think Bridget is a fallen woman," Skye announced. "On account of her name still being McQuarry, even though she was married to Mitch. I told her she ought to explain how he was a distant cousin, but—"

"*Skye,*" Bridget fretted, without turning around. It was too early to fix supper, and yet there she was, ladling bear fat into a pan to fry up greens and onions and what was left of the cornmeal mush they'd had for breakfast.

Trace came to stand beside her, her son crowing in his arms, evidently delighted at being swallowed up in a hat. "He sure does take after Mitch," Trace said. His voice was quiet, low.

Bridget didn't dare even to glance up at him. "More so every day," she agreed, striving for a light note. "I wouldn't say he's easygoing like Mitch was, though. He's got himself a strong will, and something of a temper, too."

"That," Trace said, "would have come from you."

"Skye," Bridget said crisply, as though he hadn't spoken, "go and catch a chicken if you can. And take Noah with you, please."

Skye obeyed without comment, though she might reasonably have pointed out that the two tasks just assigned were in direct conflict with each other. Noah protested a bit, though, not wanting to be parted from Trace—or, perhaps, his hat.

Then they were alone in the small, shadowy space, side by side. Bridget could feel Trace's gaze resting on her face, but meeting his eyes took some doing. Every time she looked at him, it weakened her somehow, made her want to sit down and fan herself like some scatterbrained girl at a cotillion.

"Why did you come here?" she demanded.

His expression was solemn and, at the same time, intractable. "Because I promised Mitch I would," he said. "Two days before he was drowned, he got your letter telling him Noah had been born. He was happy, of course, but it was hard for him, being so far away. After a while, he turned reflective." Trace paused, rubbed the back of his neck with one hand. "He made me swear I'd look after you, if he didn't make it home."

Bridget knew the details of Mitch's drowning— Trace had described the scene to her in a letter, his words so vivid that she sometimes forgot that she hadn't been there, hadn't witnessed the tragedy herself—but the mention of his death brought stinging tears to her eyes all the same. "Damn you," she whispered. "Haven't you done enough?"

He took the spatula from her hand and, grasping her shoulders gently, turned her to face him. "What the devil do you mean by that?" he demanded in a hoarse whisper.

"You *know* what I mean," Bridget hissed back. "If it hadn't been for you, Mitch would never have gone to war. Noah and I wouldn't have to make our way without him. How dare you come here, like some storybook knight in shining armor, when—when—"

"When it was all my fault?" he asked in that same low tone. The words were knife-sharp, for all their softness, honed to a dangerous edge.

It was no use trying to hide her tears, so she didn't make the attempt. For some reason, it seemed all right to cry in front of Trace, though she'd taken great care in the years since the war began to make sure she was alone when she could no longer control her emotions. "Yes!" she cried. "*Yes!* Mitch wasn't like you. He was guileless and sweet, and he believed everyone else was just as good, just as honest, just as kind. He would have done practically anything you asked him to, and *damn you,* Trace, you had to know that!"

Trace shoved a hand through that shaggy, light-streaked hair of his. He needed barbering in the worst way, clean clothes, and a bath, too, and for all that, Bridget felt the ancient shame, the powerful, secret pull toward him. She had never confessed that weakness to anyone, could barely acknowledge it to herself.

"Mitch had a mind of his own," he rasped. In his eyes, the ghosts of a hundred fallen soldiers flickered, one of them his best friend from earliest memory. "You make him sound like some kind of idiot. I didn't make him join the fight—he knew it was something he had to do. Hell, we all did."

They stared at each other for a long moment, like winter-starved bears fixing to tie in, tooth and claw. The air seemed to buzz and crackle at Bridget's ears, and she could feel her own heartbeat thundering in every part of her body. She told herself it was anger and nothing else. *Nothing else.*

"He had a wife and a child," she said finally. Shakily. "Granddaddy needed him on the farm. *We* needed him."

"Sweet Lord in heaven, Bridget," Trace reasoned with weary patience, "just about *everybody* had to leave something or someone behind, Federals and Rebs alike. Did you think you were the only one who made sacrifices?"

Sacrifices? What did he know about sacrifices, with his ready smile and the whole of his life still ahead of him? Bridget wanted to slap the man, but she managed to hold on to her dignity. It wouldn't do to set a bad example for Skye and Noah by resorting to violence, however great the temptation. She sniffed. "I should have known that you wouldn't accept responsibility."

He leaned in until his nose was barely an inch from hers. His eyes seemed to flash with blue and green sparks. "I'll 'accept responsibility' for anything that's my doing," he snapped, "but I'll be *damned* if I'll let you blame the whole war on me!"

"I don't see how you can stop me," Bridget pointed out. "And I'll thank you not to use profane language in my house."

Color surged up Trace's neck and flared along his beard-stubbled jaw. "You haven't changed, you know that?" And then, just as suddenly as his whole countenance had turned to fury, he grinned, all jovial good nature. "It's good to know that some things—and some people—stay the same."

Bridget was reconsidering her previous decision not to slap him. "You can't stay here," she insisted. "It's simply out of the question." She looked around at the humble dwelling, with its dirt floor and oil-barrel cookstove, perhaps a little desperately. Even the bed had been scavenged along the westward trail, left behind by some other family. "This place is hardly big enough for Skye and Noah and me as it is—there'll be talk in town—"

"I'll make camp down by the creek," he said. "And if folks have anything to say about my being here, you just send them to me." He heaved a sigh. "Now, I think I'll go out and have a look at those horses of yours, if that's all right with you."

"As if you cared one whit about my opinion on anything," Bridget huffed.

He was still grinning. It was an unfair advantage, that disarming smile of his, bright as noonday sun spilling across clear water. "I've missed you," he said, and then he turned, and when Bridget let herself look, he was gone.

Damned if it wasn't Sentinel, his own horse, penned in behind Bridget's tumbledown shack of a house. At the sight of Trace, the stallion tossed his head and ambled over to greet him with a hard nuzzle to the shoulder.

Trace stroked the stallion's white-splashed brow and spoke in a low voice. "I was afraid our paths might never cross again, fella," he confided. The goose egg on the back of his head pulsed, a reminder of the morning ten days before, when a pack of renegade Paiutes had jumped him in camp. One of them had knocked him out cold, probably with the butt of an army rifle, before he had time to think, but he supposed he ought to be grateful they hadn't relieved him of his boots, saddle, and watch while he was still facedown in the dirt. Not to mention his hair.

Sentinel blew affectionately, and Trace chuckled. "Looks like Miss Bridget's gone to no little trouble to keep you here," he observed, looking askance at the flimsy arrangement of branches and barrels posing as a corral fence. "I guess we oughtn't to tell her you could have gotten out of this with one good kick. You were waiting for me, weren't you, boy?"

Again, the horse nickered, as if to reply in the affirmative.

Trace glanced toward the house; even from outside, he could hear Bridget banging pots and kettles around. He turned his head, saw Skye and Noah chasing a squawking chicken around in the high grass, and smiled at the sight. *You did good, Mitch,* he thought. *He's a fine boy, your Noah.*

"Skye!" Bridget called. She was probably in the dooryard, but Trace couldn't see her for the cabin. "Stop that nonsense before you run the meat right off that bird!"

Trace looked heavenward. *I'll do my best,* he promised. Then he turned back to the horse and patted its long, glistening neck. "You and I, we'll just pretend we're strangers for a while," he said quietly.

The paint pawed the ground with one foreleg and flung his head, but Trace knew he'd go along with the plan, insofar as a horse could be expected to do.

Obediently, Skye closed in on the chicken and held it in both arms, and even from that distance, Trace could make out the bleak expression in her eyes. He moved toward her.

"I don't want to kill it," she confessed, and bit her lower lip. When she grew to be a woman—she was still just a girl in Trace's eyes, and maybe she always would be—she would make some lucky man an exceptional wife.

"I'll do it," he said. "You take the boy inside before he meets up with a rattler."

Skye nodded and smiled up at him with her eyes. "Thanks, Trace," she said softly, and leaned down to take Noah's small hand. Then, tentatively, she touched Trace's arm. "I'm glad you're here. Bridget is, too, even if she can't make herself admit it. You won't let her run you off, will you?"

He glanced toward the cabin, with its pitiful canvas roof. Bridget had gone back inside to slam things around some more. That woman was hell on hardware. "She always make this much noise when she cooks?"

Skye laughed and shook her head. "No, sir. That particular commotion is in your honor for sure and certain," she said, and set off through the high, sweet grass, the boy scrambling along behind her.

That night, sitting on stumps and crates under a black sky prickled with stars, they ate fried chicken for supper, along with cornmeal cakes and greens, and Trace could not recall a finer meal. He probably hadn't had home-cooked food since before he joined the army, though he'd developed a taste for it as a boy. All the while he was growing up, he'd eaten with the McQuarrys whenever he was invited, which was often. Even back then, before she picked up and left, his mother hadn't troubled herself much where such things were concerned. Tillie Qualtrough had been a loose woman, plain and simple, and she'd taken to camp following long before the war came and made a profitable enterprise of the habit.

All things taken into consideration, though, he couldn't see any sense in faulting Tillie for the choices she'd made. She'd been alone in the world, with nothing to trade on but her looks. She'd done what she had to, that was all, and despite her circumstances, which would have turned a lot of people bitter, she'd been kind-hearted and quick to laugh.

"That's a fine stallion you've got there," Trace observed, when he'd eaten all he decently could. It seemed a safe topic to him, unrelated as it was to Mitch or to his staying on at Primrose Creek. "Where'd you get him?"

Bridget's face softened at the mention of the animal; ever since she was a little girl, she'd loved critters the way some people do art or music or going to church. "I swapped the oxen for him," she said, obviously proud of the deal. "I mean to breed him to my mare, Sis, and some others and eventually start myself a horse ranch."

Trace raised his blue enamel coffee mug to his mouth, more because he wanted to hide his smile than because he needed any more of the brew. He'd be awake half the night as it was, remembering. Regretting. "I see," he said. "I guess you wouldn't consider plain farming."

She sat up straight on the crate she'd taken for a chair, her half-filled plate forgotten on her lap. "Farming," she scoffed. "This is timber country. Mining country. *Ranch* country."

"We've got a nice vegetable patch, though," Skye put in, and there was an anxious note in her voice, putting Trace in mind of somebody stepping between two opposing forces in the faint hope of keeping them from colliding. "Potatoes. Squash—" Her words fell away, like pebbles vanishing down the side of a precipice.

"You might not turn a profit for some time," Trace observed, watching Bridget. "How do you intend to eat this winter?"

He knew he'd touched a nerve, for all that she tried to disguise the fact with her trademark bravado. "We might sell some of the timber. Mr. Jake Vigil is building a house and a sawmill at the edge of town, and he'll be wanting trees."

Trace assessed the towering ponderosa pines and firs surrounding them, blue-black shadows marching as far as the eye could see, in every direction. "Doesn't look to me like he'd have any trouble getting all the lumber he wanted," he said. He didn't mean there wouldn't be a market for McQuarry timber—not exactly, anyway—but Bridget took it that way and ruffled her feathers like a little partridge, making it necessary to take another sip of coffee.

"We have flour and salt. We have a shotgun for hunting, and thanks to a friend in town, we've got enough chickens to provide eggs and"—she looked down at her food—"the occasional feast. We will do just fine, thank you."

Trace suppressed a sigh. He'd known this encounter wouldn't be easy, but he'd been afoot for the best part of a week, and before that he'd spent so much time in the saddle that for a while there, he'd thought he might turn bow-legged. He was in no mood to grapple with a stiff-backed little spitfire like Bridget McQuarry.

You promised, Mitch's memory reminded him.

Yes, damn it, I promised. And I'll keep my word.

"I'll need some timber for that roof," he said in measured tones. "You have a saw? An ax, at least?"

Bridget pursed her lips, just briefly, but she looked pretty, even in a sour pose. Motherhood lent her a softness of the sort a man can't really help noticing, no matter how hard he might try. "We can build our own roof," she said. "Skye and I will do it ourselves."

Trace rolled his eyes, but he kept a hold on his patience. Skye offered no comment but busied herself gathering up a fretful Noah and herding him inside to be swabbed down and put to bed. "And a fine job you've done, too," he said dryly, nodding to indicate the canvas stretched across the top of the house. "Roof building, I mean."

Even in the thickening twilight, he saw her color heighten. It made something grind painfully, deep inside him, seeing that. Instead of speaking, though, she just got up and started collecting the tin plates.

"Why can't you just admit that you need help?" he asked, very quietly.

She straightened, and he saw—or thought he saw—tears glimmering in her eyes. "Oh, I can admit that, Mr. Qualtrough," she said. "I've got a child and a young sister to feed and clothe. I have this house and this land and two horses and nothing else. I need help, all right. I just don't need it from you."

He sighed again. "You hate me that much?"

"No," she answered, stiffening that ramrod spine of hers. "I'm completely indifferent."

"You have to have a roof, Bridget. My being here would mean protection for Skye and Noah, if you won't accept it for yourself. And somebody has to train that stallion. You're good with horses, you always were, but you're too small to handle him, and you know it."

She was silent.

He pressed the advantage. "This is what Mitch wanted," he said reasonably. "How can I ignore that? How can you?"

The plates rattled in her hands, and she wouldn't look at him. "You'll train the stallion— put on a roof—build a barn?"

"That and more," he agreed.

She caught her upper lip between her teeth, something she'd done ever since he could remember. And that was a long time, since the McQuarry farm had bordered the little patch of no-account land where Trace and his mother had lived in what had once been slave quarters.

"No. Nothing more. You do those things, and we'll be all right. It'll ease your conscience, and you'll move on like you ought."

He stood, faced her, cupped her chin in one hand. "What are you so scared of, Bridge?" he asked. "You must know you have nothing to fear from me, not on your account and not on Skye's."

Her eyes flashed in the starlight; for a moment, he thought she was going to insult his honor by saying she *was* afraid of him, but when it came down to cases, she nodded. "I know that," she whispered. "It's just that—well, every time I look at you, I think of Mitch. I think of how he might have stayed home—"

Trace let her chin go. "Stayed home and done what?" he asked, at the edge of his patience. "Planted cotton and corn and sweet potatoes? Milked cows?"

Bridget pulled away. "There is no use in our discussing this," she said, her tone on the peevish side. Then she snatched the coffee mug out of his hand, turned, and strode toward the cabin. If the boy hadn't been asleep by then, or close to it, anyway, he knew she'd have slammed the door smartly behind her.

He watched as the lanterns winked out inside the house, first one, and then the other, and the sight gave him a lonely feeling, as if he were set apart from everything warm and sweet and good. It wasn't the first time he'd felt like that; as a boy, he'd yearned to be one of the McQuarrys, instead of some long-gone stranger's illegitimate son. During the war, far from the land and the people he knew, he'd ached inside, ached to go back to the Shenandoah Valley. After Mitch was drowned in the river that day, his horse shot out from under him, things had been a whole lot worse.

For a long time, he just sat there, mourning. Then, slowly, he turned his back on the cabin and headed for the makeshift camp he'd set up a hundred yards away, in the shelter of several tall oak trees growing alongside the creek. Rummaging in his saddlebags, he got out his spare shirt and a sliver of yellow soap. He kicked off his boots, still damp from his crossing earlier in the day, and then, downstream a little way, where he was sure he was out of sight of the house, he shed his clothes and waded, teeth chattering, into the icy waters of Primrose Creek. He made necessarily quick work of his bath, dried off with his dirty shirt, and pulled his trousers back on, his mind occupied, the whole time, with Bridget.

God only knew what she'd say when he told her they were getting married.

Chapter

2

Bridget did not receive the news with any discernible grace.

"Married?" She whooped, the next morning, as though he'd asked her to walk the ridgepole of a barn with a milk bucket balanced on her nose. She was poking around in the grass, looking for eggs and carefully setting the ones she found into an old basket. "Why, I'd sooner be tied to the hind legs of a bobcat and chewed free again."

He felt himself flush hotly, from the neck up. Some women—lots of them, maybe, given the number of men killed on both sides of the war— would have counted him good husband material. After all, he was still young at twenty-four, and he was no coward, no shirker, no stranger to hard work. He had a few dollars in good federal gold hidden in the bottom of one saddlebag, and he cut a fine figure, if he did say so himself. Once, he thought, with a rueful glance toward the pitiful corral, where the stallion watched him even then, he'd even had a pretty good horse.

She smiled, no doubt amused to see him tangled in his own tongue. "I thought you'd have started on the roof by now," she said. She shaded her eyes and looked up at the sky, assessing it as if it had something to prove to her. "We're burning daylight, you know. Breakfast will be ready in half an hour."

He swallowed hard and finally got past the lump in his throat. "I've got the ring," he said, and produced the small golden band from the pocket of his trousers as proof. It caught the early-morning sunshine as he held it up for her to see, a small and perfect circle, gleaming between his thumb and index finger.

She bent, picked up an egg, inspected it solemnly, frowned, and then threw it. It smacked against the trunk of a nearby birch tree. "You never did lack for confidence," she observed lightly, without looking at him. Her whole countenance was telling him she'd already lost interest in anything he had to say. "You can take that ring, Trace Qualtrough, and—" Just then, Noah exploded through the cabin doorway, half dressed—and the wrong half, at that—with Skye in pursuit. Bridget straightened to face Trace again. "And give it to someone else."

"I don't plan on marrying anybody else," he rasped. It was a private conversation, and he didn't want Noah and Skye to overhear. "You're going to be my wife, and I'm going to be your husband, and that, damn it all to hell, is the end of it!"

Bridget spoke through clenched teeth and a brittle smile. Skye captured Noah and hauled him back inside. "While it may be true, Mr. Qualtrough, that women have few, if any, legal rights in this country, if they can be forced into making wedding vows, I have yet to hear of it!"

He leaned down, caught the fresh-air, green-grass, lantern-smoke scent of her. Indignant as he was at the moment, and he was fit to yell, it was all he could do not to wrench her up onto her toes and kiss her, good and proper. Fact was, he'd wanted to do exactly that ever since she turned thirteen and started pinning her hair up, had even given in to the temptation once. "You're mighty choosy, it seems to me, for a woman alone in Indian country!" He'd struck his mark, he could see that by the brief widening of her blue eyes, but he wasn't proud of the victory.

"If you want a wife," she retorted, for she'd always been one to regroup quickly, "then go into town and find yourself one. Let's see—there's Bertha, the storekeeper's sister. She's twice your size, has a beard, and speaks nothing but German, but I imagine she can cook. Or maybe you'd like Shandy Wheaton. She's pockmarked, poor thing, missing a few teeth. But then, you're pretty enough for the both of you."

If he hadn't been standing right at the tips of Bridget's toes already, he'd have taken another step toward her. "Now, you listen to me. Mitch was the best friend I ever had. I would have died in his place if I'd been given the choice. He asked me to look out for you and Noah, and out here that means marrying you, ornery though you may be. So you might just as well get used to the idea, Bridget: you'll be wearing this ring before the leaves change colors!"

She glared at him for a long moment. He really thought she was going to slap him, and he would have welcomed the blow, if only because it would break the tension. Instead, she simply turned her back on him and stormed toward the cabin.

He swore under his breath, kicked up a clod of dirt, and went to the creek's edge, where he crouched to splash water on his face. The wedding band, back in his pocket, seemed to burn right through the fabric of his pants, like a tiny brand. Any sensible man would reclaim his horse, leave what money he had with Bridget, and ride out without looking back, but Trace wasn't just any man, and where Bridget was concerned, he wasn't particularly sensible, either.

Still sitting on his haunches beside the stream, skin and hair dripping, he turned his gaze toward the house, squinting against the polished-brass glimmer of the summer sun. *I've never given up on anything in my life,* he told Bridget silently, *and I'm not going to start now.*

Skye was perched on an upturned crate at the table, which had once been a spool for wire cable, her chin propped in one hand, her eyes misty with dreams. "I'd marry Trace if he asked me," she said.

Bridget hadn't told her about the ridiculous proposal; she'd evidently been spying. If the child had one besetting sin, it was that: she was a snoop.

"Nonsense. You're just sixteen—far too young to be a bride."

"You were only seventeen when you married Mitch."

"I was—" Bridget's voice snagged in her throat. *I was too young. I had a head full of dreams and fancies.* She sighed. *I wanted to keep Mitch from going to war.*

Fortunately, before Skye could pursue the subject further, Trace rapped at the door and stepped inside without waiting for a by-your-leave. Just like him.

"Mornin', monkey," he said, ruffling Skye's hair. Noah stood a few feet away, watching him shyly, but with a hopeful expression in his eyes that hurt Bridget's heart. "Hullo, cowboy," Trace said.

Noah beamed. "Hullo," he replied in a staunch little voice. "Do you have a horse? You can't be a cowboy if you don't got a horse."

Out of the corner of her eye, Bridget saw Trace's gaze slide in her direction, glance off again. "No, sir," he said, squatting down to look into Noah's face. "I reckon I can't. Need some cows, too, if you're going to be particular about it."

Noah frowned. "We got horses. Two of them. But Mama gets our milk from town, so we don't have no cows."

"We don't have *any* cows," Bridget corrected

automatically. Perhaps Noah was destined to be raised in the wilderness, with few playmates and little opportunity for culture, but that didn't mean he had to grow up to be an unlettered ruffian. She had had tutors during her girlhood on the prosperous McQuarry farm, as had Skye and their cousins, Megan and Christy, and she'd saved her schoolbooks, brought them along so she could teach her son to read and write when the time came.

"That's what I *said*, Mama," Noah replied, with an air of worldly patience. "We don't have no cows."

Trace laughed and mussed Noah's hair. Skye grinned, her eyes shining. And Bridget turned her back on all of them and made herself very busy with breakfast.

Trace dragged one arm across his brow and then glanced ruefully at the resultant sweat and grime. There ended the sorry story of his spare shirt; he'd head into town, once he'd finished sawing down and trimming the large cedar tree he'd chosen for roof lumber, and outfit himself with some new clothes. If he didn't, he'd soon have little choice but to strip himself bare, soap up his duds, and walk around in the altogether until they'd dried. The image made him grin—it was almost worth doing, it would annoy Bridget so much.

Finally, the cedar was ready to come down. After making sure no one was close by, he gave it a hard shove and watched as it fell gracefully to the ground, lushly scented, limbs billowing like a dancer's skirts. He mourned the tree's passing for a moment, then set aside the ax, took up a saw with Gideon McQuarry's initials carved into the handle, and began the pitch-sticky job of cutting away branches.

As he worked, he thought of the old man, Bridget and Skye's grandfather, and smiled. Gideon had been as much an original creation as Adam in the Garden, a tall, lanky man with eyes that missed very little and a mind that missed even less. Most of the time, his manner had been gruff, even abrupt, and yet there'd been a well of kindness hidden in that crusty old heart. Gideon had taught Trace to ride and shoot, right along with Mitch and later Bridget as well. By that time, Gideon's beloved wife, Rebecca, had passed on, and his two sons—J.R., Bridget and Skye's father, and Eli, Megan and Christy's—had fought a duel over the same mistress and accomplished nothing except to inflict each other with duplicate shoulder wounds and permanently alienate their wives. They'd gone their separate ways that very day, Eli and J.R. had, and Gideon had said he was glad Rebecca hadn't lived to see her own sons make fools of themselves in front of the whole county. Then he'd wiped his eyes on the sleeve of his shirt and turned his back to the road.

Bridget's mother, Patricia, always given to the vapors, weakened after that and eventually died. Jenny, who was Megan and Christy's mother, showed more spirit; she hooked up with a rich Englishman, applied for a divorce on grounds of desertion and disgrace, and left Virginia behind forever.

Gideon had grieved anew over that parting, not because of Jenny's going, for he'd never thought she had much substance to her character on any account, but because he feared he would never see Megan and Christy again. And he'd been right, as it turned out. When Trace had finally returned to Virginia, after a year spent flat on his back in an Atlanta hospital, recovering from a wound that nearly cost him a leg, he'd found Gideon dead and buried beside Rebecca. Eli and J.R. had been there, too, one having died for the Union cause, one for the Confederate. Bridget, long since widowed, had packed up the wagon, according to the neighbors, and headed west to Nevada, bound for a place called Primrose Creek, to claim her and Skye's share of the land Gideon had left them. The once-thriving farm, home to the McQuarry family since the Revolutionary War, had fallen into the hands of strangers.

Trace stopped swinging the ax to wipe his brow again and was grateful when he saw Skye coming toward him with a bucket and a ladle.

"I thought you might be thirsty," she said.

He chuckled hoarsely. He *was* thirsty. He was also relieved to turn his thoughts from the devastation he'd seen in Virginia. With Gideon and Mitch both dead, Bridget gone, and the big house at once forever changed and eternally the same, in his memory at least, it had seemed to him that the whole of creation ought to creak to a halt, like an old wagon wheel in need of greasing. It had been a while before he'd set out to find his best friend's wife and honor what he considered a sacred promise.

"Thanks," he said, and took a ladle full of water. He drank that and spilled a second down the back of his neck.

Skye looked as if she were working up her courage for something; he knew that expression. Skye had been tagging along behind him and Bridget and Mitch ever since she could walk. He braced himself.

"If Bridget won't have you," she said, all in a rush, "then I will."

Whatever he'd been expecting the child to say, that hadn't been it. For a few moments, he just gaped at her, while his mind groped for words that wouldn't inflict some hidden and maybe lasting wound. "If you were a few years older," he said, finally, "I'd be glad to take you up on that offer. Time you finish growing up, though, I'll just be old Trace. You'll have a dozen fellas singing under your window every night of the year."

Her lower lip trembled, and her eyes darkened. "You don't want me," she accused.

Don't cry, he pleaded silently. *Please, don't cry.* He could not bear it when a female broke down and wept.

"No," he said, because he couldn't think of anything else to say. "No, honey, I don't want you. And if I did, somebody would have to shoot me."

She bit her lower lip, looked away, looked back with a challenge snapping in her eyes. She had the same passion in her as Bridget did, he thought, the same fire. He could imagine a legion of boys and men warming up for their serenades.

By force of will, he kept himself from grinning at the picture. He took another ladle of water from the bucket, which she'd set at his feet, and drank, watching her over the enamel brim.

Skye put her hands on her hips. "You don't want to marry Bridget because of any promise to Mitch," she said. "You've loved her all along. Even when your closest friend was courting her. Even when she was his wife—"

"That will be enough," he interrupted. It wasn't true. He'd liked Bridget, that was all. And sure, he'd thought she was pretty. But love? He knew better than to fall into a trap like that.

Skye blinked, then thrust out her chin. "I saw you kiss her, the day before the wedding, in the kitchen garden."

He couldn't refute that charge; he hadn't known anyone else was around, and neither had Bridget. He'd kissed her, all right, and she'd kissed him back, and he wondered if she remembered. Though an excuse came readily to mind, that he'd merely been wishing Bridget a lifetime of happiness on the eve of her marriage to his friend, he didn't offer it. He would have choked on the first word, because he'd meant to do exactly what he did. To this day, he didn't know what had possessed him.

Suddenly, tears glistened in Skye's lashes, and she thrust out a disgusted sigh. "I'm sorry," she told him, and put a hand briefly to her mouth. "I shouldn't have said that."

"You shouldn't have been sneaking around eavesdropping on people, either," Trace pointed out.

"I was only twelve, for heaven's sake."

He chuckled.

She slumped a little. "I don't know what gets into me sometimes."

He pushed a dark curl back from her cheek, where it had gotten itself stuck in a stray tear. "I reckon it's all pretty normal," he said gently. "The time'll come, sweetheart, when you'll turn red to think of asking me to marry you, if you remember it at all."

She went ahead and blushed right then. "I'm already embarrassed," she said, and sat down on a nearby tree stump. "You're not going to tell anyone, are you?"

"Our secret," he promised.

She was visibly relieved, and her smile was tremulous and beautiful, like sunshine after a thunderstorm or candlelight flickering in the dark. "You're a good man. Why doesn't Bridget see that?"

"She'll come around," he said.

"Do you love her?"

Trace wondered if a tactful McQuarry had ever drawn breath. He doubted it. "I feel something. Maybe it's friendship. Maybe it's regret, because she lost a husband and I lost a good friend. Whatever it is, I reckon it might grow into love, given enough time."

Skye plunked her knobby elbows on her knobby knees and rested her chin in both palms, regarding him carefully. "Bridget cried, you know. After you kissed her that day in Grandma's garden, and she sent you away, she sat down on that old stone bench and cried till I thought I'd have to let on that I was watching and put my arm around her or something. Then Granddaddy caught me looking and pulled me back into the house by my ear. He told me that eavesdroppers always hear ill of themselves, and I had to help Caney peel potatoes all afternoon." Caney Blue was the family cook; she, too, had been gone when Trace got back to Virginia. To that day, he thought of the spirited black woman whenever he came within smelling distance of hot apple pie.

"He was quite a man, your grandfather."

Skye sighed. "I miss him so much. He was more like a daddy than Daddy ever was."

"I know," Trace answered gently. Gideon had been a father to him as well, in all the most important ways.

"You know what he was trying to do, don't you? Leaving half this land to Bridget and me and half to Christy and Megan?"

Trace nodded. "It was the greatest sorrow of his life, except for losing your grandmother, to see his family torn apart the way it was. You and Bridget and Christy and Megan have the same blood in your veins, whatever your differences might be. Gideon wanted the four of you to patch things up and get on with your lives, so he left you this land, probably figuring you'd have to get along if you were neighbors."

Skye nodded, but a melancholy aspect had overtaken her. "I don't reckon our cousins will ever come back from England. They've probably got all sorts of beaus and pretty dresses and hair ribbons." She paused, sighed dramatically. "I bet they go dancing every single night."

Trace allowed himself only the slightest smile. "Is that the sort of life you'd like to live, monkey?"

She pondered the question. "Sometimes I think it is," she confessed. Then she shrugged. "Other times, I just figure I want to stay right here forever." She took in the incredible vista of mountains and timber by spreading her arms, as if to embrace it all. "This place is beautiful, don't you think?"

It wasn't gentle, rolling Virginia, but Nevada had a magnificence all its own. It was a new place, made for a new beginning. "Yes," he said, and meant it. "This is as fine a land as God ever turned His hand to."

Quicksilver—with Bridget-like speed—Skye's agile mind careened off in another direction.

"We didn't even know Granddaddy owned these twenty-five hundred acres."

Trace thought back. "I don't recall that he ever mentioned the place."

"The lawyer said he got them when an old friend defaulted on a debt. I guess that cabin we're living in now must have belonged to that poor man, whoever he was." She stood, with a resigned sigh, and smoothed her skirts. "I'd better get back. Bridget wants to work with the horse, and I promised to look after Noah so he won't try to help."

Trace had bent to put the ladle back in the bucket, and he was reaching for the ax handle when Skye's announcement stopped him in midmotion. "What did you say?"

"I said—"

"Not the stallion," he said quickly. Damn, he should have warned them. He should have told them that Sentinel had been mistreated by his last owner, that he had injured at least half a dozen seasoned cowboys, that only he, Trace, had managed to win the animal's trust. "She wouldn't try to work with the stallion?"

"Sure she would," said Skye, sounding baffled by the question. "Why would she want to train Sis? She's been riding that mare ever since Granddaddy gave it to her for her fifteenth birthday."

Trace was already running toward the house, his mind full of bloody, broken-bone images, leaping over fallen logs, nearly landing on his face when he caught the toe of one boot under a root, and half deafened by the sound of his own heartbeat drumming in his ears. Sentinel was a fine horse, the best, but he was dangerous and bad-tempered, too. That was surely why those thieving Paiutes had been willing to trade the critter for a pair of worn-out oxen; they hadn't been able to tame him, either. And if a pack of Indians, every one of them riding from the time they could hold on to a horse's mane, couldn't break the paint to ride, Bridget certainly wouldn't be able to do it.

"Bridget!" he yelled, as he sprinted across the meadow toward the house. Sure enough, she was standing by that matchstick corral, with a halter draped over one arm. Noah was beside her, holding on to her skirt and peering up at the horse.

She turned at the sound of her name, and, of all things to notice at a time like that, he took in the fact that she'd done something to her dress, sewn a V right up the center of the skirt and snipped it away to fashion a trouser-like get-up. He shouted her name again.

She watched him for a few moments, as though she thought he might flap his arms and take flight or something, then turned and shooed Noah away from her side. One small finger caught in his mouth, the boy went reluctantly toward Skye, who was following Trace at a much slower pace.

Bridget moved the branches that served as fence rails and approached the stallion, raising the halter. Sentinel danced backward and tossed his head. Even from that distance, Trace could see that the beast's eyes were rolled upward in either fury or panic. The last time the horse had looked like that, he'd caved in a man's rib cage with his front hooves and would have killed him if Trace hadn't interceded.

"Bridget!" Trace roared. He felt as he sometimes did in dreams, as though he were running in mud. Working hard and getting nowhere.

She turned to look at him again, and the stallion reared against the sky, his forelegs slicing at the air, and let out a long, whinnying shriek that turned Trace's blood cold as creek water.

No, he screamed, only to realize that he hadn't spoken at all. Hadn't made a sound. *No.*

When Sentinel brought his hooves down, he missed Bridget by inches. Then he reared again and sprang like a jackrabbit, straight over Bridget's head, racing wildly toward the creek. She fell, and, for a heart-stopping moment, Trace thought she'd been struck after all. Noah scrambled toward his mother, screaming, and he and Trace reached her at the same instant.

No blood. She was looking at him. Blinking. Pale.

She sat up to draw the boy into her arms and whisper into his gossamer hair. "Hush, now, darling. I'm not hurt. I'm fine." She met Trace's gaze over Noah's head and repeated herself distractedly. "I'm fine."

Trace, on one knee in the grass, felt like shaking her. At the same time, he would have given anything to pull her close and comfort her the same way she was comforting Noah. Well, sort of the same way.

"Are you out of your mind?" he spat. "That horse could have—"

"But he didn't," Bridget interrupted softly. "Catch him for me, Trace—bring him back. Please?"

He'd never been able to deny her anything, not even when they were kids, and she knew it. "We are not through talking about this," he snapped. But then he got to his feet and went after the stallion.

He found the animal a mile downstream, high on the opposite bank, caught in a blackberry thicket. Trace spent an hour freeing the frightened horse, then led him into the water to wash off his scratched legs and pick out half a dozen more thorns. All the while, he scolded the stallion, but his voice was quiet and even, and when Trace headed back toward the cabin, Sentinel followed him, docile as an old dog.

Bridget was waiting in the dooryard, one hand shielding her eyes as she watched man and horse cross Primrose Creek.

"How did you do that?" she asked, none too graciously, either, for somebody who had done a damn fool thing like trying to put a halter on a half-wild horse.

Trace set his back teeth before answering. His boots were full of water, his pants were soaked to his thighs, and he'd nearly lost the woman he'd sworn to protect, not to mention a perfectly good stallion. He was not in a cordial state of mind. "How," he drawled, "did I do *what?*"

She retreated half a step, though she probably wasn't aware of it. "You're angry," she said. It might have been a marvel, if you went by the surprise in her voice.

"You're damned right I'm angry," he growled. "Fact is, I'm *so* angry that it would be better if you and I didn't talk just now."

"But—"

"Bridget, if I get started yelling, I don't rightly know when I'll stop again," he said, and went way out around her. Sentinel ambled along behind him, nickering a cheerful greeting as they passed the mare.

There was no sense in putting the stallion back in Bridget's corral, so Trace drove a stake into the ground and used his rope as a tether. Then, since he still didn't dare open his mouth around Bridget, he headed back to the cedar tree and swung the ax with a new vigor.

He was drenched in sweat and nearly ready to collapse when he became aware that he wasn't alone. Expecting to see Skye with another bucket of water, he was caught off-guard when he found himself facing Bridget again.

"I've made dinner," she said quietly. "You must be hungry."

He ran an arm across his mouth, inwardly testing his temper. He figured he could speak without raising his voice. "Yes," he said. Better to err on the side of caution.

"Thank you for fetching back my horse."

Trace had to bite his tongue, figuratively anyway, to keep from correcting her on the point of ownership. "We had an agreement, Bridget. *I'm* supposed to train the stallion, remember?"

She wrapped her arms around her middle, as though chilled, and sighed. "How do you do it, Trace? How do you—well—make a friend out of a wild horse the way you do?"

He felt a stab of guilt, but it was quickly quelled. If he admitted that Sentinel was his horse, he realized, she'd believe him, but she would be furious, and there would be one fewer reason for him to stay on at Primrose Creek. Her pride, at once the taproot of her strength and the source of many of her sorrows, might even prevent her from accepting further help of any sort. If he left, there was a very good chance that she and Skye and little Noah would either freeze or starve over the coming winter. Or get themselves carried off by Indians.

"I don't know how I do it," he replied honestly. "It's a knack, I guess. Gideon used to say I was part gypsy." He gave a rueful, tilted grin and shrugged slightly, thinking of his scandalous birth. "For all I know, he was right."

Her cornflower-blue eyes widened a little; he sensed a softening in her and feared it was pity. There were things he wanted from her, it was true—

their old easy camaraderie, for example—but not sympathy. "Do you ever wonder about him? Your father?"

He shook his head and folded his arms, perhaps to form a barrier of sorts. He wasn't sure. "No." That was a lie, of course. He'd wondered about him a thousand times and even asked Gideon if he knew who the man was. And Gideon had laid one big, callused hand on his shoulder and put his greatest hope and worst fear to rest in the space of two sentences. *"I'm not him,"* he'd said. *"Nor is either of my sons."*

"I heard my daddy and my uncle Eli talking about him one day. Your father, I mean. They said he was a Northerner." She paused, lowered her eyes, then met his gaze squarely. "He was killed in a bar fight when you were little."

Trace's jaw hardened painfully, and the pit of his stomach knotted. "You knew that? All this time, you knew, and you never told me?"

She spread her hands. "How could I? You had all these grand visions of how he was going to come back and marry your mother—"

He turned his back on her, on the dreams of a lonely little boy. Flinched when he felt her hand come to rest lightly on his shoulder.

"Do you think we could start over?" she asked softly. "Oh, Trace, we were such good friends once upon a time—"

Such good friends. He'd have cut his heart out of his chest and handed it to her, if she'd asked it of

him. Ironic that Skye, sixteen and innocent, had
been the one to see into the dark passages of his
soul with perfect clarity, and thereby forced him to
see, too. If he hadn't loved Miss Skye McQuarry
like a sister, he would have been furious with her.

"Trace?"

He made himself face Bridget, put out his hand.
"Friends," he said, and all the while, he was con-
scious of the wedding band in the depths of his
pants pocket—where it was likely to remain.

The truce held until after the midday meal, when Trace announced that he was going to town and wanted to take Noah along with him. He'd borrow the mare, if Bridget didn't mind.

She didn't mind, not about the mare, anyway. Letting her son out of her sight, however, was evidently another thing entirely. Bridget, seated on an upturned crate across the table from Trace, straightened her spine with the same dignity she might have exhibited at home, presiding over Sunday dinner at her grandmother's fine mahogany dining table. "My son will stay right here," she said, her blue eyes snapping with challenge. "Primrose Creek is a tent town, full of saloons and inebriated drifters and loose women. Let me assure you, it is no place for a child."

Skye groaned right out loud at this pronouncement, and, out of the corner of his eye, Trace saw Noah's face fall with disappointment. If it hadn't been for those factors, he might have laughed at Bridget's statement. "The boy was born smack in the middle of a war," he pointed out reasonably. "He made the trip out here, none the worse for wear. And I hardly think you need to concern yourself that he might take up with 'loose women'—not just yet, anyhow."

Bridget glared at him. Obviously, she did not like discussing the subject of a visit to Primrose Creek in front of her son, but he wasn't about to back down without a tussle. Noah didn't belong only to her, he belonged to Mitch, too. And Mitch, Trace knew, would not have wanted his boy brought up to be timid, particularly in a place that demanded strength and courage of a person, be they man, woman, or child.

"The subject," she said, "is closed."

Trace stood up. "I'm going to town, and Noah is going with me." It was all a bluff, because if Bridget held her ground, he wouldn't override her wishes, but the issue was an important one, and he could be every bit as stubborn as she was. "I reckon we'll be back before you manage to have me arrested." With that, he carried his plate and fork to the wash basin, deposited them there, and started for the door.

Skye looked from her fuming sister to Trace and back again. "I want to go, too," she said. There was a note of shaky determination in her voice, and she stood. "May I go with you?" she asked Trace.

He nodded and extended a beckoning hand to the boy. Waited.

Noah hesitated, reading his mother carefully, then edged toward Trace.

Bridget stood, blushed furiously, and then sat down again. "I'll expect you back here before sundown," she said.

"You could come with us," Skye suggested quickly. Trace could tell that the girl wanted to walk over and lay a reassuring hand on Bridget's shoulder, but she didn't move. "It's not far to town. You and I could walk. Maybe pick some wildflowers for the supper table—"

Bridget merely shook her head, and though she said nothing more, the look she gave Trace just before he turned away said plainly that the fires of hell itself could not surpass what she would do to him if anything happened to Noah or Skye.

Outside, he saddled the mare and helped Skye to mount, hoisting Noah up to sit in front of her. She looked confused. "I don't mind walking, Trace," she said. "I walk all over the place, all the time." She bit her lip briefly, averted her eyes for a moment, and Trace guessed by her guilty manner that she'd been to town on her own, probably on more than one occasion, with Bridget none the wiser. "I mean—"

"I know what you mean," he said sternly. "You go ahead. I'll ride the stallion."

Her eyes went wide. "But he's not even halter-broke—"

"We have an understanding, he and I," Trace said easily. Then, using Bridget's rope halter in place of a bridle, he swung up onto Sentinel's bare back and urged him forward with a feather-light motion of his knees.

Skye's mouth was wide open. "I'll be jiggered," she said. "That horse is close kin to the devil, and here you are riding him like he was a pony at a fair!"

Trace laughed. "Come on," he replied. "You heard your sister. If we're not back here by sundown, she'll hang my hide out like a hog's and scrape off the bristles."

He'd gotten a look at the settlement of Primrose Creek the day before, passing through on his way to find Bridget and the boy, but he hadn't lingered long. It was typical of mining and timber towns all across the West, with whiskey flowing free and good sense at a premium. Even armed with a .44 as he was, a man was at a distinct disadvantage without a horse under him; Trace never ran from trouble, but he wasn't one to seek it out, either.

"You stay close to me," Trace told Skye, as they both dismounted in front of the general store, a building with a temporary air about it, as though it might be planning to pick itself up some dark night and go sneaking off into the countryside. The merchandise—as well as the clientele—was visible through the cracks in the walls.

Skye nodded and turned to help Noah out of the saddle, only to find him with one small foot in the stirrup, set on getting down on his own. It gave Trace an odd sense of pride, witnessing the enterprise, as though he'd had something to do with the making and raising of this boy.

Trace waited, held out a restraining arm when Skye would have taken her nephew by the waist and set him on his feet. Then Noah was standing on the ground, gazing up at him with an expression so reminiscent of Mitch that, for a moment, his throat closed up tight. After a hard swallow and a long study of the horizon, Trace was able to look down into those bright, eager eyes again. "Now, you listen to me, boy," he said, not unkindly, but at the same time making it clear that he would brook no nonsense. "You don't go wandering off anywhere. You and I, we're partners, and we've got a lady to look after. That means we have to stick together."

Skye rolled her eyes. "I come here all the time," she hissed.

"If I catch you at it," Trace answered under his breath, "I'll paddle your backside."

Skye colored, and that reminded him of her sister. No telling how long Bridget would hold this little escapade against him, for all her pretty words about what good friends they'd been back in the old days.

"You wouldn't dare," Skye said.

"Try me," Trace responded.

The general store turned out to be remarkably well stocked for such a rustic establishment: there were blankets and boots and ready-made shirts and good denim pants, made to last. While Skye admired a shelf full of books, handling one and then another as reverently as if they'd been printed in letters of fire on Mount Olympus, and Noah squatted to brush aside some sawdust and set a red and blue striped top to spinning on the floor, Trace selected two sets of everyday clothes and set them on the counter, which was really only a pair of rough-hewn boards stretched between two fifty-gallon barrels.

The storekeeper, a burly gray-haired man with a wiry white beard, smiled broadly and greeted him in a strong German accent. Trace couldn't help thinking of the woman Bridget had mentioned, the one twice his size, and wondering if he'd get a look at her. He figured a female who didn't speak English might not be a bad bargain; a man could get some peace, keeping company with somebody like that. Unless, of course, she talked as much as most women did. It was bad enough when you could understand what they were saying. Being nagged in another language would be worse still, because there'd be no way to fight back.

"Something else for you?" the storekeeper asked, interrupting Trace's runaway train of thought. He'd said his name was Gus.

Trace indicated Skye and the boy, both lost in pursuits of their own. "We'll be wanting that toy," he said. "And one of those books, into the bargain." He paused, thought of Bridget again, remembered how she'd loved to curl up in the porch swing on a hot summer afternoon back home in Virginia and lose herself in some story or another. Times like that, he and Mitch hadn't been able to coerce her to ride or fish or climb trees with them, no matter what they said or did.

He smiled at the memory of a time when Bridget's life—all their lives—had been simple. Safe. "Better make that two," he added.

Gus beamed, pleased, and gestured toward the shelf. "You choose, yes?"

"Yes," Trace agreed, and stepped up beside Skye. "Which one?" he asked in a quiet voice.

She looked bewildered. "Which—?"

"Which book, monkey," he prompted with a grin. "Or don't you accept presents from men who turn down your marriage proposals?"

Her cheeks turned a fetching shade of pink, but she smiled. "Presents? But it isn't Christmas or anything—"

He sighed, examined the titles. For a place like Primrose Creek, the selection was impressive; obviously, not all the miners and lumbermen spent their wages on whiskey and women. "Go ahead," he said. "You can have any one you want."

She took a blue clothbound volume off the shelf and clutched it to her chest as if she thought he might change his mind and take it away. He chose a second book, one with a bright red cover and gold print on the spine; it was a love story, and there was a horse in it. Just the kind of thing Bridget would enjoy.

"We—we had to leave Granddaddy's books

when we came out here," Skye told him, and he was touched to see tears in her eyes. "All we brought with us was the Bible, the one that's got all the McQuarrys' names written inside, clear back to the first war with England. Bridget said we had to take useful things, food and blankets and warm clothes and the like—"

Trace touched her nose with the tip of his finger. "It must have been real hard, leaving home," he said.

She nodded, blinked, and looked away.

He understood about that and gave her the time and privacy to collect herself while he selected other things from the shelves: flour, yeast, sugar, coffee, and all manner of other staples. After making arrangements for Gus to bring the foodstuffs as far as the creek's edge in his buckboard, they left the general store.

A portly middle-aged man wearing a nickel-plated star on his vest was admiring the stallion. "Fine horse you've got here," he said. "Care to sell him?"

"No," Trace answered, too quickly. Then, "You'd have to speak to Bridget McQuarry is what I mean. It's her horse."

The marshall put out one hand. "My name's Flynn. Sam Flynn. I don't believe I've seen you around Primrose Creek up to now."

"Trace Qualtrough," Trace replied. "I just got here yesterday."

Flynn assessed him thoughtfully. "You just passing through?"

Trace shook his head. "I mean to tie the knot with the Widow McQuarry," he said. Might as well spread the word; it was bound to happen, after all, and folks would find out eventually, anyhow.

The lawman chuckled. "Well, now," he said. "That will come as bad news to the gentlemen of our fine town." He glanced apologetically at Skye and tugged at the brim of his hat, and Trace could have sworn the older man colored up a little, under all the beard stubble and hard experience. "I hope you don't think I meant any disrespect for your sister, miss," he went on. "It's just that she's got plenty of admirers around here, whether she knows it or not."

Skye nodded. Her eyes were twinkling when she looked at Trace. "Sounds like you've got some competition," she said.

About that time, Noah lifted one foot over a puddle of horse piss and stomped.

Skye wrinkled her nose, scooped the boy up, and set him in the mare's saddle. "Now, look at you," she fretted. "You're getting a bath as soon as we get home, Noah McQuarry. And, phew, you stink."

Trace grinned. The boy smelled, and that was a fact, but such escapades rarely proved fatal. "Glad to meet you, Marshal," he said, and, after tying the string-bound parcel containing his new clothes, the books, and Noah's top behind Sis's saddle, swung up onto Sentinel's back.

"Looks as if you might be a fair hand with a horse," Flynn observed. "There's work around here for a man who knows one end of a critter from the other."

"I've got a roof to build," Trace replied. "After that, though, I might be looking to make wages."

The marshall raised a hand in farewell. "I'll see that word gets around. Not that folks haven't already noticed you're here, of course. Don't wait too long on that wedding, Mr. Qualtrough. We're mostly men here in Primrose Creek, but there are a few ladies who've come to save our sinful souls. One or two of them might take it upon themselves to make judgments."

Skye glowered. "Those old crows," she muttered. "They'll be lucky to save their *own* souls." Trace had heard her, and he was pretty sure the marshal had, too. The lawman's smile confirmed it.

Trace grinned back. "I'll keep your words in mind," he promised, and then they headed toward home. They crossed the creek just as the setting sun was spilling crimson and orange and deep violet light over the cold, shallow waters.

Bridget was standing in the dooryard with her hands on her hips. She looked both testy and confounded; testy because she'd probably expected them to spend half the night reveling in one of the tent saloons, confounded because Trace was riding the stallion she believed to be untamed.

"Noah needs a bath," Skye said immediately. "He stepped—*stomped*—right into a puddle of—" She paused. "Well, a puddle. And Trace bought me a book, all my own. Noah got a top, and——" She glanced back at Trace, caught the look he gave her, and fell silent. He supposed she was both grateful for the book and afraid he'd tell Bridget that she'd been to Primrose Creek before on her own.

Bridget laughed and shook her head when she caught a whiff of Noah. "Put some water on to heat," she told her sister cheerfully. "I'll scrub him down before supper."

Skye nodded and, after collecting the precious parcel from behind the mare's saddle, led the boy inside. Bridget took a light hold on the cheek piece of Sis's bridle, and, for what seemed a long while to Trace, he and Bridget just gazed at each other.

It was Bridget who broke the silence. "Noah had a good time," she said quietly. "I haven't seen his eyes shine like that since——well, since last Christmas at Fort Grant, when one of the soldiers carved a little horse for him."

Trace waited. When Bridget had something on her mind, it was better to let her have her say, all in one piece.

"He's missed having a man around," she went on, and he could tell she'd swallowed her pride, that she wanted to look away and wouldn't let herself. "I was just——I was so afraid. Of his going to town, I mean. I don't think I could bear losing him."

"It's all right, Bridget," Trace said, and, swinging one leg over the stallion's glistening neck, slid to the ground. "Noah's your son. I shouldn't have brought up the subject of going to town in front of him—it wasn't fair—and I'm sorry for that." He was standing very close to her now and wondered how he'd gotten there, since he had no memory of the steps in between. She smelled of green grass and clear creek water and supper, and her proximity filled him with a sweet, mysterious ache, partly pain, partly glory, that he did not choose to explore. "Mind you, I still think it's wrong to shelter the boy too much. Mitch wouldn't like it."

She let that pass. "You've been kind to Skye, as well as to Noah. I'm grateful for that."

He nodded an acknowledgment, held his tongue. He couldn't think of anything he wanted to say that wouldn't get her all riled up again, like as not, and he just didn't have the stamina to hold his own in a skirmish. They just stood there, for a long moment, looking at each other, thinking their own separate thoughts.

"I'll tend to Sis," she finally said, and walked away, leaving him standing there, staring after her. She had already removed the mare's saddle and bridle and left her to graze in the high grass before he took a single step. He might not have had the presence of mind to do that much if the stallion hadn't butted him between the shoulder blades and damn near knocked him to his knees.

Gus, the storekeeper, appeared on the far side of the creek, despite the settling twilight, waved a meaty hand in cheerful greeting, and began unloading boxes and bags from the back of his buckboard. Bridget smiled somewhat nervously and started toward him. She didn't have the money to pay for supplies, and she didn't dare take anything on a note of promise. She might very well need to run up a bill over the winter months, and it was vital to keep the ledger clear in the meantime.

Since Gus's last name was unpronounceable, nobody ever used it. It made for a unique sort of slap-dash familiarity that would have been improper in most any other place or situation. "Gus," she called, stopping at the edge of the creek. "What are you doing?"

"I bring you groceries, missus," he said. His face was round as a dinner plate, and his eyes were a bright, childlike blue. His white beard made him resemble St. Nicholas. "I could carry them over, but my sister, Bertha, she don't like the night dark. I got to get back to her."

Bridget was at a complete loss, but not for long. "But I didn't order groceries."

He set the last box on the rocky ground, and the buckboard tilted dangerously when he climbed up to take the reins. Bridget's heart went out to the gray mule in the harness; Gus must have weighed almost as much as he did. "Your feller, he make business with Gus. Good night, missus."

"But—"

"I tell Bertha you say hullo," he called, already headed back toward town. He didn't even turn around, just waved one big hand again, this time in farewell, and drove on.

Trace, after eating a light supper of bread and cold chicken, had gone back out to hack at the fallen cedar tree, taking a lantern along to provide the necessary light, and Skye, having washed the dishes and sung a freshly bathed Noah to sleep, was settled at the table, her head bent over the book Trace had bought her. Bridget did not want to walk into the woods—the prospect of time alone with Trace was simply too disturbing—and she wasn't about to drag Skye away from her reading.

Never one to leave work undone if there was a spare minute in her day, she sat down on the bank, unlaced her shoes, and removed them, along with her stockings. Then she tied her skirts into a big knot, roughly on a level with her knees, and waded into the creek. No sense leaving the food where it might be stolen.

One, two, three crossings, and then she was finished, and Trace was standing at the edge of the yard, watching her. She hadn't heard him approaching, hadn't seen the lantern. A guilty thrill rushed through her, seeming to come up from the ground, through her body, out the top of her head, because her legs were bare. Quickly, but not quickly enough, she untied the fabric of her skirt and shook it into place, as glad of the darkness as she'd ever been of anything. He had surely seen her limbs, but he didn't need to know about the heat in her face and the strange riot among her senses.

"You shouldn't have done this," she said.

"What?" he asked. His voice was hoarse, and he sounded honestly puzzled.

"You shouldn't have bought all this food. I can't repay you, and I don't like being obliged."

He sighed. "You're not obliged, Bridge," he said. "I'm your friend, remember? I believe it was only this morning that we agreed on that."

She couldn't be angry with him. He was generous; it was his nature. Besides, he'd made Skye and Noah so happy. "Yes," she said. "We agreed." He handed her the lantern, bent to lift one of the crates with an exaggerated grunt. "You carried this stuff across the creek? Remind me not to arm wrestle you."

Bridget laughed. "Oh, I will. If indeed the subject ever comes up."

He carried the box inside, set it on the floor beside the stove. He refused any help, over Bridget's protests, and went back for the others. Bridget occupied herself putting the treasures in their right places—sugar, coffee, flour, salt. Tea. Spices and butter. Dried peas and salt pork. Canned meats and vegetables. Two bars of soap, one for laundry, one for bathing. Kerosene for the lamps. It had been so long since she had had such luxuries, all at once, that she was very nearly overcome.

Skye didn't look up from her book even once during the entire interlude, and that made Bridget smile. She, too, had missed reading, missed it desperately. She'd been through the Bible twice since leaving home—skipping Leviticus and Lamentations both times, with apologies to the Lord—and she was ready for a story she hadn't heard, read, or been told beside a campfire. Perhaps, when Skye had been through that lovely clothbound volume of epic poetry two or three times, she would make Bridget the loan of it.

She became aware of Trace very suddenly, knew he was standing just inside the cabin, though she had neither heard nor seen him after he brought in the last box. A moment passed before she thought it prudent to turn around and face him.

He was there, just where she knew he'd be, his fair hair golden in the light of the lamp Skye was reading by.

Guilt swamped her, for surely the things she was feeling were sinful, especially when all tangled up with the deep and private fury he roused in her. She thought, God help her, of what it would be like to tell him her secrets, to cry, at long last, because Mitch and Granddaddy were both dead, and her home, her heritage, her birthplace, was gone forever. She wanted to confess that she'd been scared—no, terrified—more times than she could count, but she hadn't shown it, hadn't dared, because Skye and Noah had no one to depend on but her. Not even the day those Paiutes came, riding their short-legged, shaggy ponies, armed with bows and arrows and hatchets. She'd nearly swooned when she'd looked up from the clothes she was washing in the creek to see them on the other side of the water, watching her with fierce, expressionless faces.

She'd been so frightened that she hadn't even noticed the paint stallion they were leading, magnificent as he was. All she'd been able to think of was her sister and her son and all the dreadful stories she'd heard about women and children at the mercy of savages.

Then one of the men had ridden across the water and indicated the oxen, the two tired beasts who'd pulled the wagon all the way from Virginia to the mountains of Nevada, with a thrust of his spear.

"Take them," she had said. "If you want them, take them." She'd given Skye strict orders to stay out of sight if the Indians ever came, no matter what happened, to take Noah and climb out over the low place in the back wall and hide in the root cellar until she was sure it was safe to come out. Despite Bridget's explicit instructions, Skye had walked right up to Bridget's side, bold as you please, and solemnly handed her Granddaddy's shotgun. And scared as she was, Bridget had thought to herself, *She's growing up.* Then, *Oh, God, please—let her grow up.*

The Paiutes had looked askance at the shotgun, and little wonder. They were equipped with army carbines, in addition to their knives, bows, and spears. They'd spoken to one another in a quick, clipped, and guttural language, and then they'd laughed.

Bridget had cocked the shotgun. Told them to take the oxen and get out.

Miraculously, they complied, and when they went, taking the oxen with them, they left the stallion behind. . . .

"Bridget?" The sound of Trace's voice brought her out of the disturbing reverie.

She blinked. "Oh. Yes. Yes?"

"I just wanted to say good night." Dear heaven, but he was a fine-looking man; he had always been half scoundrel, half archangel, and that had never changed.

She wet her lips and deliberately remembered Mitch. How he'd loved her. How he'd trusted her. How he'd died to defend her and Noah and all the things he'd believed in. "Good night," she said, barely breathing the word, and then the door was shut fast, and he was gone.

Bridget swallowed hard and wondered why she wanted to cover her face with both hands and weep inconsolably. To distract herself, she walked over to Skye and laid a hand lightly on her silken brown hair. "It's time to rest," she said softly. "Besides, you'll spoil your eyesight, reading for so long in such poor light."

Skye looked up, blinked. Made the transition from the world inside the pages to the one around her, the roofless cabin, the bed she shared with both Bridget and Noah, when at home she'd had a large room all her own. They all had, Skye, Christy,

Megan, and Bridget herself. Oh, but everything had been so different before the war. Everything.

"What?" Skye asked.

Bridget bent to kiss the top of her sister's head. "Time to put out the lamp and go to bed," she said. "Morning will be here almost before you close your eyes."

Skye sighed dreamily. "Do you suppose Megan and Christy have ever seen a real knight? Being in England, they might have—"

Bridget smiled. "I suppose so. But I don't think knights wear shining armor these days."

Her sister sighed again, though this time she sounded a little forlorn. "I wish we had knights. Here in Nevada, I mean."

Oddly, Bridget thought of Trace, almost said there might be one or two around. Wearing ordinary clothes, of course. Building roofs and training wild horses. "Silly," she said, and laughed. "You'll meet a nice man, when the time is right, and you won't care *that*"—she snapped her fingers—"about knights in England."

Skye looked miserable. "I asked Trace to marry me today," she said.

Bridget was taken aback. "Oh, Skye."

"I thought if you didn't want him, well, I'd take him. I mean, I think he's nice, and he's handsome, too."

Bridget was careful not to smile. "And what did he say?"

"That I'm too young. That I'll have men singing

under my window someday, and that if he said yes, he ought to be shot."

Bridget bit the inside of her lower lip. "I see." She went toward the bed, unbuttoning her bodice as she walked. "Well, I'd say he was right on all counts. You are too young. You will have all manner of suitors. And I would most certainly have shot him. Come to bed, Skye. You'll have time to read tomorrow, after the chores."

"Do you think he's handsome?"

Bridget had stopped talking, stopped thinking, stopped breathing. There was a book lying on her pillow, a red leather book with golden print embossed on the cover. "Wh-what did you say?" she asked. She must have started drawing in air again at some point, she reasoned, or she wouldn't have been able to speak. Her hand trembled as she reached out for the treasure.

Skye had put out the lantern and was now standing on the opposite side of the bed, pulling on her nightdress. In the spill of moonlight seeping through the canvas roof, Bridget saw that her sister was smiling.

"He bought that for you," she said. "It's a present. I thought I'd die, waiting for you to notice."

Bridget's knees felt unsteady; she turned her back to Skye, sat down on the edge of the mattress, one hand to her mouth, the other clutching the book to her chest. She hadn't looked at the title, had no idea of the subject, but it didn't matter. It was a *book*. Tears brimmed in her eyes.

"It's a love story," Skye whispered, climbing carefully into bed, lest she awaken Noah. "Very tragic. There's a horse, and somebody dies. I'm not sure who, though I don't imagine it's the horse. It will make you cry, though."

Bridget said nothing. She was, after all, already crying, but there was absolutely no point in calling attention to the fact.

Trace, her heart called, through the darkness that separated them. *Oh, Trace.*

Chapter

4

Trace had already carried water in from the creek and gotten the fire going in the stove by the time Bridget opened her eyes the next morning. Skye and Noah were still sleeping, Skye fitfully, Noah with a sweet-dream smile touching just the corner of his small mouth.

"Morning," Trace said, quiet and gruff-voiced. It wasn't yet dawn, but his grin flashed like light off a mirror. "I was beginning to think you meant to pass the whole day right there in bed."

Bridget knew he was teasing, but she was mildly chagrined all the same. She arose quickly, pulled on her worn wrapper, and stepped into her shoes without fastening the buttons. The dirt floor was always cold until the sun got a good start, and she wasn't one for going about barefoot, anyway. There were too many perils, from sharp stones to snake-bite, and a simple puncture wound from a nail or other rusted object might bring on lockjaw.

She shifted her thoughts to the bracing aroma of hot, fresh coffee scenting the crisp predawn air. She knew without looking that there was dew on the grass, for the sun was still mostly huddled behind the hills to the east, and the ground was surely hard and cold. She felt a pang of guilt for her lack of hospitality, necessary though it was.

"Did you sleep well?" she asked, taking a sip from the mug of coffee he'd poured for her.

Trace's mouth tilted upward at one corner, but his eyes were solemn, in a gentle, uncomplaining sort of way. "I've slept in worse places than green mountain grass, Bridge," he assured her.

She was filled with a swift, consuming desire to know all his experiences, large and small, and told herself it was because what Trace had endured, Mitch had, too. "Where?"

He drew a deep, slow breath and expelled it slowly. "In rocky fields. Inside the trunks of trees, under them on the ground, and up in the branches. Barns and burned-out houses and, once or twice, a chicken coop."

Bridget had already wrinkled her nose and grimaced before she realized the expression could be construed as rude. "A *chicken coop?*"

Trace chuckled, a man-sound that Bridget had sorely missed after he and Mitch and Granddaddy had all gone. "It wasn't so bad," he reflected, and this time, there was real humor in his eyes. "Fact is, we counted ourselves lucky to bunk there, given that the sky was dumping icy rain and there wasn't any other shelter for about ten miles in any direction."

She felt a small crinkle form between her eyebrows. " 'We'? Was Mitch with you?" It was so important to know, though she couldn't have explained why in a month of full moons.

He nodded. "Mitch and nine other men." A distant look entered his eyes, threw shadows. "One of them was bleeding pretty bad. We tried to keep him alive, but he was gone by morning."

Bridget touched his forearm. "I'm sorry, Trace."

"It's all right," he answered. "It's all right," he said again. But then he turned his back and went to the door to watch the sunlight spill over the waters of the creek. Bridget knew that was what he was doing because it was a spectacular, sometimes even dazzling sight, and she'd done the same on many a morning herself.

She didn't cross to him but busied herself with the assemblage of breakfast—cornmeal mush, molasses, one of the precious tins of pears Trace had bought in town the day before at Gus's mercantile. "Thank you for the book," she said, shy as a schoolgirl acknowledging a valentine. She wondered what it was about Trace that kept her off-balance, sometimes bold, sometimes reticent, and always confused. Why, if she hadn't known better, she might have thought . . .

No.

He didn't turn around, and the cool breeze felt good, filling the cabin with sweet freshness and a multitude of sounds—birds singing, the creek telling its old, old story, the horses greeting one another in snuffles and muted whinnies.

Bridget felt a swell of love for the place, rising up from the core of her being, and all of a sudden, she knew that however much she missed Virginia—and the memory of it would always be a tender bruise pressed deep into her heart—Primrose Creek was home now. She set the cast-iron kettle on top of the stove, hoisted up one of the buckets, and filled the pot with water. She was making no effort to be quiet now, for there was work to be done, and Skye's help would be needed.

"I was glad to do it," Trace said belatedly. "I'll see to the stock while you and Skye are getting dressed." With that, he was gone.

Skye grumbled something from the direction of the bedstead, and Bridget smiled to herself. Skye was not at her best in the mornings. Noah, on the other hand, was wide awake from the instant he opened his eyes, and he was already bouncing in the middle of the straw-filled mattress.

"I didn't wet!" he crowed. "I didn't wet!"

"Good thing for you," Skye grumbled. More than once, they'd had to carry the mattress outside to air in the sunshine.

"I'm proud of you, Noah," Bridget said.

By midmorning, Bridget and Skye were toiling in the vegetable garden, and Trace's ax echoed rhythmically through the woods. Noah was sitting on the ground, spinning his top on the surface of a flat rock, and the sun was high and hot.

"Mama?" Noah said in a tone of gleeful wonder, and in the odd stillness that followed, in the space of a single heartbeat, Bridget heard it. A brief, ominous, hissing rattle. She raced toward her son, stumbling over furrows and flailing through waist-high stalks of corn, and it seemed as though she traveled a great distance in that flicker of time.

A small rattlesnake was coiled on the ground, just to Noah's left. Bridget didn't reason, she didn't scream; she simply acted on instinct. She snatched up the snake in her right hand, feeling a fiery sting midway between her wrist and elbow as soon as she did so, and hurled the creature away, into the pile of rocks to one side of the garden. The bite on her forearm burned like a splash of acid; a sickening heat surged through her body, brought out a clammy sweat. Nausea roiled in her stomach, and the ground tilted at wild angles.

"Take him inside," she gasped to Skye, swaying a little but keeping her feet. "Take Noah inside. Now!"

Skye obeyed—she was a sobbing blur to Bridget by then—and ran stumbling across the clearing, battling through brambles and high grass, shrieking Trace's name.

Bridget pulled off her sunbonnet and tried to make a tourniquet of sorts with the ties. Then she leaned over and threw up in the dirt.

Trace appeared in the throbbing, thundering

void, lifted her into his arms, carried her inside to the bed.

"Lie still," she heard him say. His voice seemed to come from the far end of a long chimney pipe or the depths of a well. "Just lie still."

Bridget closed her eyes, felt herself slipping toward the darkness, and opened them again. She could not, *would not* die. Noah needed her. Skye needed her. Devil take it, she needed herself.

Trace was not part of the equation—or was he?

"It hurts," she said.

"I don't doubt that," Trace said. "And I'm about to do something that's going to hurt more. Shut your eyes, and do your best to relax."

She tried but got no further than the shutting-her-eyes part; before she could follow through and relax, something hot and sharp sliced into the swelling wound where the snake had bitten her. She swooned, for the first time in her life, and found sanctuary in the cool gloom of some strange inner landscape.

Trace loosened the tourniquet on Bridget's upper arm; he'd replaced her bonnet strings with his leather belt. He'd drawn as much of the poison as he could, and now came the hardest part. The waiting.

"Will she die?" Skye whispered. She didn't worry that Noah would overhear, for the boy had curled up on the bed beside Bridget, close as he could get, and fallen asleep. It was as though the child thought he could save his mother by holding on tight.

"No," Trace said, and it was a vow before God. "No. Bridget isn't going to die."

"It happened so fast," Skye murmured, gazing at her sister with fear-glazed eyes. "I don't know why she didn't use the hoe. She's killed a lot of snakes since we took to the trail."

"I don't reckon she took time to consider her choices, honey. She was thinking about Noah." He sat down carefully on the edge of the bed, took one of Bridget's still, pale hands in his. The sight and feel of the calluses on her palms and fingers jabbed at his awareness, made an ache behind his eyes. She'd been reared to be a lady, the well-bred and educated wife of some prosperous Virginian, with servants at her beck and call, linen sheets on her bed, fine china and silver gracing her table. Instead, she'd wound up in a broken-down cabin, all but alone in the middle of Indian country, with a lifetime of hardship and struggle ahead of her. "Is there any whiskey around here?"

Skye glared at him and set her hands—which were probably just as work-worn as Bridget's—on her hips. "No," she said, peevish. "And this is no time to be drinking anyhow, Trace Qualtrough. I don't know what you could be thinking of."

He would have laughed if he hadn't been so afraid Bridget would never open her eyes. "It's good for cleaning wounds," he told her gently. "How about carbolic acid? Or quinine?"

She shook her head. "No," she fretted, "and there's no doctor in Primrose Creek, either. Gus might have some medicine at the mercantile, though."

The store had been well stocked, Trace reflected. He was pretty sure he'd gotten most of the venom out of Bridget's snakebite, but he didn't like to leave her. Her forehead was hot as an oven brick, and it wasn't a good sign, her not waking yet. Nonetheless, he shook his head and replied, "I'll go. You stay right here next to Bridget. Talk to her, so she knows she isn't alone." *So she won't slip away.*

Skye cast a glance toward the open door. "No," she said. "No, *I'll* go—I'll take Sis and be back in no time at all."

"Skye—" Trace began. He wasn't inclined to argue. Skye was a vulnerable young woman, and Primrose Creek was a dangerous place.

She'd backed all the way to the threshold. "You can't stop me," she said. And then she bolted.

He should have chased her, brought her back, he knew, but he was bound to Bridget somehow, as surely as if there had been a short but strong cord stretched taut between them. "Be careful," he muttered, and set his jaw when he heard Skye and the little mare crossing the creek with a lot of splashing, yelling, and whinnying.

Then he laid the back of his right hand to Bridget's forehead and thought, couldn't help thinking, what it would mean to lose her. In the hard years since he and Mitch had ridden away to war, he'd sustained himself with the simple knowledge of Bridget's existence, recalling the sound of her laughter, the fire of her temper, the deep blue of her eyes. To him, she'd symbolized everything good about home. Whatever the distance between them, real and figurative, he'd carried her with him every step of the way, a secret saint hidden away in his heart.

"Don't go," he whispered.

Her lashes fluttered, and she murmured something, but she hadn't heard him. She was wandering through the red mists of a fever, he knew, perhaps lost, seeking a way out. She would live if she could, no doubt of that. Bridget McQuarry might have been a little thing, small-boned and fragile-looking as a canary bird, but she had the spirit of a Roman warhorse.

He brushed his lips across the backs of her knuckles and settled in to keep his vigil.

She dreamed she was back in Virginia. It was twilight, and the cicadas and fireflies were out. A jagged shard of moon hung in the sky, transparent as a thin layer of mica, and the collapse of the Union was still far off, a troublesome possibility, a topic men discussed after supper, while they smoked their cigars and drank their brandy.

Bridget sat in the swinging bench on the veranda; she heard the familiar creak of the supporting chains as she rocked and dreamed. It was getting chilly, but she didn't want to go inside, not yet. She wrapped her arms around her middle and went on savoring it all: the scent of the lush flower garden her late grandmother had started as a bride, the distant lowing of the cows, and the nickering of horses. The house, a three-story structure of whitewashed wood, with green shutters at each of its many windows, brimmed with light and noise and family behind her—she heard her cousin Christy pounding doggedly at the ancient organ in the parlor, heard Skye and Megan chasing each other through the downstairs rooms, squealing with delight.

And Mitch was beside her on the swing, hidden in shadow, holding her hand. She was completely happy in those moments, though even then she knew that the sturdiest of blessings could be snatched away in the blink of an eye.

She had only to think of her grandmother's passing to be reminded that life was a fleeting and oft-times frail gift. Rebecca had gone riding one perfect summer morning, and when Bridget saw her again, Granddaddy was carrying her across the meadow toward the house, tears shining on his face. Something had spooked Rebecca McQuarry's prize gelding; she'd been thrown and struck her head on a stone. She was already gone when Granddaddy and Uncle Eli found her.

"Bridget?"

She started a little; she'd thought Mitch was beside her, there in the swing, but the voice belonged to Trace Qualtrough. She fidgeted with the soft organza of her dress. Where was Mitch?

He took her hand, Trace did. "Don't go," he said.

Her heart flailed, like a wounded bird trying to take wing. She picked up the ivory-handled fan lying in her lap and stirred the air in front of her face, for it felt uncommonly warm all of the sudden. "Go? Don't be silly, Trace. Where would I go?"

His hold tightened on her hand, a firm grip but not a painful one. "There's nobody I care about more than you, Bridget," he said. "God help me, it's always been that way."

She frowned, but something caught up her spirit and carried it skyward in a dizzying rush. Her heart pounded, and the fan picked up speed. She started to speak, had to clear her throat and start again. "You don't mean it."

"I do mean it. Right or wrong, it's so."

Didn't he know she was going to marry Mitch? That had always been understood. Mitch needed her; he'd said so himself, a thousand times. She was his strength, she was his soul. She was his honor, and all his courage came from her. He could not imagine a life without her at his side.

"Mitch," she said, a little desperately. "I've got to marry Mitch. I promised."

"You don't love him. You know you don't."

It was true, Trace was everything to her that she was to Mitch, but she could not allow that to be so. She'd long since decided that. "No," she whispered. "Please—no."

If he'd kissed her then, she would have been lost, but he didn't. He touched her hand to the side of his face, held it there lightly for a mere moment and for the length of eternity, and then he stood up, said good night, and walked away without looking back.

And there would be another time when he didn't come back. A time when she needed him more than she ever had or ever would. A time when he'd failed her.

"Bridget?" She didn't open her eyes, though he sensed that she was beginning to awaken. Skye had gone to town and returned with both whiskey and carbolic acid, bought from Gus on credit, and Trace had treated Bridget's wound with the latter several times, in the hope of staving off infection. Her skin had blazed with heat all day, but now, with evening creeping across the land, shadow by shadow, a deep chill had seeped into her, and that scared Trace more than the fever had.

"She's not getting better," Skye breathed, "is she?" She looked stricken, and little wonder. Bridget was surely one of the cornerstones of her life: sister, mother, friend. "She's—she's shivering."

Trace nodded. Then, on an impulse, he wrapped Bridget in bed quilts, gathered her up in his arms, and carried her over to the stove. There he sat, rocking her back and forth, staring down into her face with fierce concentration. Willing her to hold on.

Skye made supper, fed Noah, put him to bed, and lay down beside the child in her clothes.

Trace did not relinquish his hold on Bridget but held her through the night.

It was almost dawn when, at last, she opened her eyes, blinked, and stared at him with something resembling amazement. "The snake——?" Terror seized her; she struggled to sit up. *"Noah!"*

He held her firmly. "Noah is fine," he said. "You're the one who was bitten."

She gnawed at her lower lip, and he could see that she was debating with herself: believe, don't believe. "My son—where——?"

"He's sound asleep. He and Skye."

She let her head rest against his shoulder, and even though he knew it was weakness, not affection, that made her snuggle in close like that, he treasured the sensation. He'd come so near to losing her.

"Are you hungry?" he asked. He might have had sandpaper in his throat, the way he sounded.

She shook her head. Then, very softly, "You saved me, didn't you?"

He grinned; couldn't help it. She was *alive*. "I wouldn't put it that way, exactly. There's still some swelling, and I reckon you're sore as all get-out, whether you'll admit as much or not. You're going to have to rest for a few days."

She blinked, stiffened in protest. "A few days?" she echoed. He might have said she'd never walk again, if you went by her tone. "That's impossible! There's the gardening to do, and the cooking——"

He laid a fingertip to her lips to silence her. "We won't starve, Bridget."

"But winter is coming, and—"

"And I'm here. So is Skye. You could still get in trouble with that bite if you don't take care of yourself. Where would Noah and Skye be then?"

That gave her pause, though it was obvious that she wasn't one bit pleased at the prospect of giving in.

As a lady of leisure, in fact, Bridget was hopeless. She let Trace put her in bed and cover her up, let Skye bring her tea and Noah tell her stories, but her eyes were big and frightened, and in between long slides into healing sleep, she fussed and fretted.

Trace worked all day, cutting wood for the roof, but he came in often to check on Bridget. Skye looked after Noah, and the two of them weeded the garden and carried water and kept Bridget company whenever she was awake.

Trace took a bath in the creek at sundown, put on clean clothes, and went into the cabin. Skye had made a simple but flavorful hash for supper, and he managed to pester Bridget into taking a couple of bites. There were big dark circles under her eyes, and her skin was bluish-pale, like thin milk. He knew she was in pain, knew also that he would never hear her say so. The bite was still angry, but the swelling was going down, and there was no sign of infection.

He made a brew of hot water, molasses, and

whiskey and brought it to her. It had a lot more kick than tea, and it might dull the pain a little.

She sniffed the concoction and scrunched up her face.

"Drink it," Trace commanded. He wanted to reach out, brush a tendril of pale gold hair back from her forehead, but that would be pushing his luck. She was skittish as a filly about to be ridden for the first time, and the mere suggestion that she might need anyone's help—his in particular—was bound to scare her half to death.

She took a cautious sip, coughed, tried to push the mug back into his hand.

"Drink," he repeated.

"Where are Noah and Skye?" She was stalling.

He took the cup, held it gently to her mouth. Reluctantly, she sipped and swallowed. "They're right here, darlin'. Sitting at the table, playing cards." Poker, to be exact. He'd taught them himself—well, he'd taught Skye, anyhow; Noah still had a way to go—while Bridget was asleep, but it was probably better not to go into too much detail just then. He grinned at her, made her drink more and then more of the whiskey mixture, but slowly.

"Trace?" She'd taken half the drink, and she was already getting heavy-eyed.

"Um?" He set the cup aside, tucked the covers under her chin.

"Thanks."

He leaned down and kissed her lightly on the

forehead, the same way he might have kissed Skye. The result was a tangle of emotions and sensations that fairly took his breath away, though he was pretty sure he'd managed to hide his reactions. "Anytime," he replied. "But I'll thank you not to go grabbing up any more rattlers."

Her eyes shone, though she could barely keep them open. "You'll be—you'll be close by?"

He wanted to kiss her again, but he didn't dare because he knew it wouldn't be the same kind of kiss as before. So he nodded instead. "I brought my bedroll in and laid it out over there by the stove. Go to sleep, Bridget. You need to sleep."

A smile wobbled on her mouth, vanished. "I *hate* to sleep," she said.

He knew it was true. She was a vital person, energetic, fully alive. Even her stillness was vibrant, and she begrudged every idle moment. "Look at it this way," he teased. "The sooner you go to sleep, the sooner it will be morning."

She managed a small, strangled laugh, and he knew he'd turned a corner, that somehow his whole life had pivoted on that tiny sound. "That's what I tell Noah," she said.

He raised an eyebrow. "Well, then," he said, "it must be true."

She smiled again and closed her eyes, none too soon. The tenderness he felt toward her was overwhelming, bound to show in his face, and he didn't want her to see it, lest she retreat again.

*   *   *

When Bridget awakened the next morning, a burning ache throbbed in her arm, but she would have celebrated if she'd had the strength. She was alive, thanks to Trace. On the crate next to the bed, a fruit jar spilled over with colorful wildflowers, reds and violets, yellows and whites, and the new book was there, too, promising so much.

The tarp had been drawn back from the roof, halfway at least, and Trace, shirtless and sweating, grinned down at her from the rafters. "Hullo, Sleeping Beauty," he said.

She swallowed hard. Trace had been twelve or so the last time she'd seen him without a shirt; she'd come upon him and Mitch down at the swimming hole. This was disturbingly different. "What are you doing up there?"

Even from that distance, the mischief was clearly visible in his eyes. "Now, what kind of question is that?" he countered. "I'm fixing to put on that roof I promised you."

She felt self-conscious, lying there in bed, gazing up at Trace and his naked chest. "Put on a shirt," she said, sitting up. "You'll get sunburned."

Again, that lethal grin. "Watch out," he warned. "You keep talking like that, I might get the idea that you care."

She blushed. "Stop looking at me. How on earth am I supposed to get up with you staring at me like that?"

He laughed. The sun shone around him like an

aura. "You're not," he said. "Supposed to get up, I mean."

Bridget sighed. "In the meantime, you plan on nailing up beams and shingles right over my head?"

He pretended to consider the matter seriously. "I guess we'll have to put you outside, by the creek." Again, that light in his eyes. That grin. "Skye and I have rigged up a place."

The mere thought of getting outside raised Bridget's flagging spirits. She smiled. "Really?"

"Really," he replied, and dropped into the cabin, agile as some sort of jungle creature. "If you're ready, I'll take you out there right now."

Bridget couldn't help staring at him, and she was mortified by her own wantonness. What kind of woman was she, looking at a man's bare chest? A man, no less, who was not her husband.

Not Mitch.

He seemed to read her thoughts, and a sad smile rested on his mouth and settled in around his eyes. He lifted her out of bed, quilts and all, and somehow managed to hand her the book he'd bought for her in town a few days before. The breeze and sunlight were like the touch of a healing hand, and Bridget gasped in delighted surprise when she saw the hammock. He'd tied an old blanket securely between two small but sturdy birch trees, a stone's throw from the creek's edge. Skye and Noah were further down the bank, each holding an improvised fishing pole, and both of them beamed when they saw Bridget.

It was heaven, lying there in that hammock, shaded by the dancing shadows of leaves, lulled by the sound of flowing water. Bridget read, dozed, and read again. Noah and Skye continued to fish, and Trace worked on the roof, driving in wooden pegs with Granddaddy's hammer.

"Look, Mama!" Bridget had nodded off, but the sound of her son's voice and the feel of something cold and slick against the back of her hand brought her awake. "I caught a fish!" he crowed.

Sure enough, Noah had a fine, gleaming trout on the hook. She laughed and leaned over to kiss his cheek soundly. "Why, it's nearly as big as the whale that swallowed poor Jonah," she observed.

Noah nodded. "Nobody helped me, neither. I did it all by myself."

Bridget ruffled his shining hair, thought of Mitch. Some of the sparkle faded from Noah's catch, from the sun-spattered creek, from the comforting sound of Trace's roof building. "Your papa would be so proud," she said softly.

Noah's small brow knitted into a frown. "I want Trace to be my papa," he said.

The remark didn't surprise Bridget, but it did sting. "Sweetheart," she said, fighting a silly, weak impulse to break down and cry. "Oh, sweetheart. Things don't work that way. Your papa was a man named Mitch McQuarry, and even though he's gone, he'll always be your father."

Noah let the fish fall to his side, and there was something so disconsolate in the motion that Bridget yearned to gather him in and hold him close. She restrained herself, though; Noah might be a small boy, but he wasn't a baby. To patronize him would serve no purpose but to undermine his dignity. "Where is he? My papa, I mean?"

"We've talked about that before, Noah," Bridget reminded him. She had to look away, dash at her cheek with the back of one hand. "He's in heaven."

"Is he coming back?"

She met her son's gaze. "No, darling. People like to stay in heaven when they get there. It's a wonderful place."

"Could we go there? You and me and Skye and Trace? Could we go and find my papa?"

Bridget swallowed, glanced at the creek, and made herself look at Noah again. Her eyes were still dazzled; she could not make out his features. "All of us will go there, someday," she told him carefully. "But not anytime soon." *And not together.*

Noah digested that. "Oh," he said. Then, quicksilver, he held his gleaming trout high above his head again and whooped, "Look, Trace, I caught a fish, all by my own self!"

5

Marshal Sam Flynn showed up the next day, stood with his head back and his thumbs hooked into his gunbelt, squinting as he admired the new roof on the McQuarry cabin. "Yes, sir," he called to Trace, who was straddling the ridgepole. "That's a fine job of work. Jake Vigil sees that, he'll be after you to turn a hand to that sawmill he's trying to get built."

Bridget had mentioned a sawmill, but Trace had seen no sign of one during his brief visit to Primrose Creek the day he'd bought the groceries. "He got a planer?" Trace called back. He had plenty of rough timber. What he needed was lumber, cut to measured lengths and planed smooth, if he was going to get Bridget's place in any kind of shape; besides the roof, she needed bedrooms added on, and a barn. A real corral.

"Steam-operated," Sam answered, sounding as proud as if the machine were his own. "Has one

coming, anyhow. I reckon it's someplace between
here and San Francisco. Jake's got a good bit of
lumber laid by, though. Had it planed over in
Virginia City. He might be willing to make a trade
for some labor."

Trace reached for his shirt, discarded earlier
when the sun was high, stuck the handle of the
hammer through his belt, and made for the edge of
the roof. From there, it was an easy jump to the
ground. "I'm obliged, Sam," he said, and thrust out
a hand.

The marshal shook it. His horse, an overfed
sorrel with ears like a mule's, snuffled behind him.

Trace grinned. "This a social call, or did my
wasted youth finally catch up to me?"

Sam chortled. "If you got a wasted youth, it's
bound to turn up on your doorstep one of these
days." He swept off his sweat-stained hat and
thrust the splayed fingers of his left hand through
thinning hair. "Fact is, though, I came out here to
bring a letter for Mizz McQuarry. Come all the
way from England, and from the looks of the envelope, it's been one hell of a trip."

Trace frowned as he accepted the thin scrap of
translucent vellum. Bridget had been recovering
from the snakebite for a full week, and although he
knew she'd enjoyed being waited on and fussed
over for the first few days, she did not have the
temperament to be an invalid. In fact, she was as
cantankerous as a mother bear missing a cub. Trace
cherished a slight hope that the letter might cheer

her, but at the same time, he knew it must have come from one or both of her estranged cousins, whom she viewed as virtual deserters.

He slapped the letter thoughtfully against his palm. "Water your horse, Sam, and sit a spell." He indicated the upended rain barrel he'd taken off the broken-down Conestoga while scrounging for tools. By then, the wagon had somehow gotten itself overturned on a steep hillside, and it wasn't good for much of anything now besides firewood. Bridget was probably asleep, and he knew she'd kill him if he invited the marshal inside while she was in repose. He'd been treading carefully around her, in order to preserve the delicate peace, and neither one of them had ventured to mention his proposal of marriage. "I'll let Bridget know you're here."

"I can see that for myself," Bridget said clearly, and he turned to see her standing in the cabin doorway. She'd put on her yellow calico dress and caught her long, long hair back at the nape, and she looked thin and pale and incredibly young. "Come inside, Mr. Flynn. I'll make some coffee."

Sam doffed his hat and smiled, but Trace could see that the other man had taken note of Bridget's malaise. "I'm obliged, ma'am," he said, "but I can't stay. I just came to bring this here letter. Got some rowdies in town, and I don't want to leave them to it for too long."

She managed a smile, but she was holding the door frame with one hand, as though unsteady, and the blue shadows under her eyes made Trace want to go off in search of a doctor. He'd just decided that he'd drag one back from Virginia City if he had to when she answered. "I can't imagine who'd be writing to me," she said.

"Come all the way from England," the marshal said, for the second time. "I hope it brings you good news, ma'am."

Bridget's smile had already faded. "England?" she said, and started toward them. She stopped uncertainly in the middle of the dooryard. Sam, busy hauling himself up into the saddle, didn't see the expression on her face, but Trace did, and he almost wished he didn't have to give her the letter.

He went toward her, placed the envelope in her hand, and supported her by slipping an arm loosely around her waist.

She studied the elegant, faded handwriting, the stamp, the words *McQuarry Farm* and *Virginia* crossed out, replaced with *Primrose Creek, Nevada.* "It's—it's from Christy," she said. He couldn't tell much from the tone of her voice, but her lingering weakness gave him worry enough to last a lifetime. "She—she must have thought we were all still at the farm—"

"Come inside, Bridget," Trace said firmly, after sparing a wave for the departing marshal. "You'll be wanting some privacy, and you need to sit down."

She allowed him to steer her back into the cabin and seat her at the table, and that, too, was troublesome proof of her frailty. Skye and Noah were somewhere nearby, fishing for trout, and the house was quiet. She'd shown a fondness for tea since her encounter with the snake, and Trace went about brewing a batch, using a plain cooking pot to boil the water while she sat there, staring at the letter as if she thought it might sprout wings and fly out the window.

"Our parting was not a pleasant one, you know," she said, so softly that he almost didn't hear her.

"I know," he replied quietly. "I was there, remember? People change. Situations change."

Bridget was silent for a long time, and when she spoke, it was as if she hadn't heard a word he said. Didn't recall that he'd helped haul the two of them apart. "We had a dreadful row, Christy and I, that last day. Things were said—"

He would have crossed the room and laid a hand to her shoulder, if he hadn't guessed that she didn't want to be touched. "Maybe it's time to forget old differences. Family is family, after all."

She was watching him; he felt her gaze, in that uncanny way, even before he turned and met her eyes. "Uncle Eli went with the Confederate side. Christy said our daddy, Skye's and mine, was a traitor for taking up the Union cause. Said he was a disgrace to the whole state of Virginia and ought to be hanged."

Trace sighed. "Bridge," he said. The water wasn't quite hot, but he dumped a couple of spoonfuls of loose tea in, anyhow. "She was a kid. You were a kid. The country had just snapped in two like a dry twig. A lot of folks said a lot of things they didn't mean."

She bit her lower lip, reached for the letter, lying travel-worn on the table before her, drew back her hand again. "I told her I hated her, Trace," she said. She closed her eyes tightly for a moment, and when she opened them again, her gaze was fixed on something far away. "I spat on her skirt."

"If I recall it correctly," he said, "you went at her with your claws out. She gave as good as she got, and I suppose the two of you would have killed each other if your granddaddy and I hadn't dragged you apart."

She blushed. Set her jaw. "I vowed I'd never forgive her," she said.

He leaned down, peered doubtfully into the can of hot water and floating tea leaves, and stirred the concoction once with a wooden spoon. "Some promises," he answered distractedly, "really ought to be broken." He knew immediately that he'd made a mistake, but it was too late.

"Yes," she said. "Like the one you made to Mitch, for instance."

"That," he replied after a beat, "was different."

She thumped her fingers lightly on top of the letter; that was still as close as she'd gotten to opening the thing. One eyebrow was raised, and there was a triumphant tilt to one corner of her mouth. "I'm not so sure of that," she said thoughtfully, but she didn't pursue the subject any further.

He was grateful for her restraint; as it was, he felt like a trout wriggling on a hook about half the time. Not that he'd have left, no matter how good a case she made. She had to marry somebody sooner or later, and it might just as well be him.

He sloshed some of the tea into a mug and set it before her. "I'll be on the roof," he said, and headed outside.

She looked into the mug, furrowed her brow, and then smiled to herself. "Make sure you wear your shirt," she said. "You'll be peeling like an onion if you don't be careful."

He sighed, winked somewhat dispiritedly, and left the cabin.

Bridget waited until Trace was overhead again, hammering away at the shingles he'd fashioned from thick pieces of tree bark. Although she wasn't quite ready to tell him so outright, she was glad he was around. If he hadn't been there when she was bitten by that rattler, she would surely be dead, and Skye and Noah would have been left alone.

Skye was strong, in her own way, and resourceful; she would have found a way to provide for herself and her nephew, but Bridget shuddered at the predicament the girl would have been in—a woman's options were narrow, after all, especially in a place like Primrose Creek. She could enter into an immediate and probably loveless marriage or trade her favors for food and shelter; the line between those two situations was thin indeed. Thanks to Trace, though, Skye could grow to full womanhood and choose a husband for herself when the time came.

You're stalling, Bridget scolded herself. Then, with her hands trembling a little, she picked up the envelope, turned it over, and broke the once-fancy wax seal covering the edge of the flap.

The single page inside bore an embossed crest in the upper left-hand corner, and beneath that was a date—approximately six months before— and *Fieldcrest,* the name of Christy and Megan's stepfather's estate.

Bridget sniffed once and gave the sheet of fine paper a nearly imperceptible snap before reading on.

Dear Bridget,

I direct this letter to you because I know you must be managing everything and everyone around you, like always. My regards to Skye.

Word of Grandfather's death reached us just this morning. His lawyer wrote to inform us of his passing, or we would not have known. I should have expected to hear such news from you—had you been anyone else at all.

According to Grandfather's man-of-law, Megan and I have inherited half of a tract of land he referred to as Primrose Creek, way out in the West somewhere, with the other half going to you and Skye—as well, it would seem, as the farm itself and all of Grandmother's lovely things.

In any case, having no use for such a distant and desolate expanse, my sister and I would like to sell our share of the property. We have expressed our wishes to Grandfather's representative in Richmond, but following a long discussion, we came to the decision that it was only honorable to offer our acreage to you before turning to strangers. We would expect a fair price, of course.

Please reply at your earliest convenience. Both Megan and I are eager to make plans.

Sincerely,
Christina McQuarry

Bridget might have crumpled the missive and flung it across the room if it hadn't been the second or third letter she'd ever received. A muddle of emotions simmered and stewed within her—anger at some of the things Christy had implied, sorrow that her once big family had been so diminished, the very real fear that her cousins would sell the land on the other side of the creek to someone who would cut off the water supply somewhere upstream, or chop down all the trees to sell for timber, or scrape away the topsoil to dig for silver, gold, or copper. . . .

"You got a letter?" The voice was Skye's.

Bridget looked up, blinked. Her sister was standing in the doorway, and the light came from behind, leaving her face in shadow. "Yes," she said, a little wearily, and took a cautious sip of Trace's tea. "Where is Noah?"

"He's on the roof with Trace," Skye said. Then, quickly, "And don't start worrying. Trace tied a rope around his middle."

Bridget rolled her eyes. Better not to think about that just now. "It's from Christy," she said, and held out the letter.

Skye was at her side, snatching the page from her fingers, in a fraction of a moment. "Holy boot grease," she said.

Bridget let that pass. "They want to sell their share of the land," she said, unnecessarily, for Skye was probably on her second pass through the letter by then. "Somehow, we've got to raise enough money to buy it."

Skye sank onto her customary crate, just to the left of where Bridget sat. Overhead, the hammer thwacked, and Trace and Noah carried on a running conversation. "How are we going to do that?" she asked.

It was a more than reasonable question. It had taken practically everything Bridget had, everything she could sell or swap, beg or promise, just to get this far. She had no money, none at all, and Grandmother's silver teapot and jade brooch, the last of their inheritance, had gone for last winter's room and board at Fort Grant. "I don't know," she confessed at some length. "But I'll find a way."

Skye watched her intently. "There aren't many folks willing to live way out here," she said.

"Probably, that land will just stay empty, like it is now."

It wasn't *entirely* empty; there had been an Indian village on that site, long ago, and an ancient lodge still stood on the hillside opposite the cabin, hidden from view by a stand of birches, oaks, and cottonwoods. "It's fine land, Skye. Someone is going to want it. And what if it's the wrong some-one?"

Skye said nothing. They both knew that certain sorts of neighbors might well represent a danger to them, once Trace had done his self-imposed penance and moved on. And Bridget had no doubt that he *would* move on, when the old restlessness set in. For that reason, and several others, she must not allow herself to care for him.

Carefully, Bridget folded the page, returned it to its envelope, got the McQuarry Bible out of its square pine box, and tucked the letter inside. When she turned around, she caught Skye watching her with a thoughtful smile.

Bridget pressed her lips together, smoothed the skirts of her calico dress, and went outside to shade her eyes with one hand and look up. Noah was wielding the hammer, his tongue pressed into one cheek, while Trace supervised. It was an ordinary scene, a man and a boy working together, but the sight filled Bridget with a strange, bittersweet poignancy. In one and the same moment, she wished Trace had never come to Primrose Creek and rejoiced that he had.

He looked up, probably expecting her to demand that he bring Noah down from there *this instant,* and she wanted to do just that, wanted it the way parched ground wants water, but she held her tongue. Made herself go inside.

By suppertime, Trace's back, chest, arms, and shoulders were painfully red and hot to the touch.

"I warned you," Bridget fussed, getting out the jug of cider vinegar she kept for flavoring dandelion greens and the like. "Wear your shirt, I said. But you're so hard-headed, and you just wouldn't listen—"

He laughed, though it was perfectly obvious that he was suffering. "I figure if I go down and lie in the creek for a while, I'll be fine."

"You'll take a chill, going from one extreme to the other like that," she said. "Sit down, and let me tend to you."

He looked at the vinegar and the handkerchief she'd gotten from the trunk she and Skye used in place of a bureau and narrowed his eyes dubiously. "Is that going to hurt?"

"Now is a fine time to ask that," Bridget responded.

He flinched when she dampened the handkerchief and touched it gently to the broiled flesh on his left shoulder. "You seem to be feeling better," he said. "Nothing like tormenting me to brighten your day."

She shook her head but could not maintain her serious expression. She laughed. "I *warned* you," she reminded him. "You're going to be sore for a couple of days, Trace, and you'll be lucky if you sleep tonight."

He was looking at her; his eyes were turquoise in the fading light. They'd had supper—fresh trout and greens and some of Skye's rock-hard biscuits—and the cabin had taken on a cozy aspect, what with the new roof and the lamplight and the lingering aroma of a good dinner. Skye and Noah were sitting together on the high threshold, watching the first stars come out.

"I'll be going into town again tomorrow," he said. "I want to speak to Jake Vigil, see if I can swap for some good lumber. Build a corral and some shelter for the horses."

She nodded; her throat felt thick, for some odd reason, and anything she tried to say would have come out as a croak.

"I was wondering if you wouldn't like to go along," he went on. He was not a shy man; Trace had always been the boldest of the three of them, dreaming up all sorts of mischief and then cajoling Mitch and Bridget into going along. And yet there was boyish uncertainty about him now, arousing an unwelcome tenderness in Bridget. "Just for an outing, I mean."

A refusal sprang to the tip of her tongue, but she bit it back. Both Skye and Noah had turned in the doorway to watch her, plainly awaiting her answer, and the truth of it was, Bridget was sick and tired of staying at home. She would assess the growth of Primrose Creek for herself, find out if there was a church yet, and a bank. Most definitely a bank.

"Yes," she said. "I'd like that."

Trace had gone back to sleeping by the creek, making a bed of the hammock he'd fashioned for Bridget's convalescence, and he reached for his shirt as soon as Bridget had finished dousing him with vinegar, pulled it on gingerly, leaving the buttons undone. Bridget had been able to avoid looking at his chest throughout the exercise, but now, all of a sudden, it drew her gaze, once, twice, a third time.

She finally had to turn away. "Good night, Trace," she said.

He was close behind her, so close. She felt his warm breath caress her nape. "Good night," he answered.

The storm rolled in after midnight, sundering the sky into blackened pieces, shaking the new roof over their heads. Lightning illuminated the landscape with an eerie clarity, and the horses shrieked in terror. Commanding Skye to stay inside with Noah, Bridget pulled on her wrapper, slipped her feet into unlaced shoes, and dashed out. Just across the creek, a giant ponderosa pine exploded into flames, flaring up like a torch.

Bridget turned, stumbled around the house to the corral, where Sis was kept, the stallion being tethered some distance away. The mare was in a frenzy, running back and forth in the small space, flinging her head, screaming and sweat-soaked.

"Easy, girl," Bridget said. "Easy."

She could hear the stallion between claps of thunder, but she knew Trace was with him.

Sis, probably recognizing Bridget's voice, or perhaps her scent, calmed down slightly. Nickered.

"Come here, Sis," Bridget said, holding out a hand to the frightened animal. "It's me. See? It's Bridget. And I'm not going to let anything happen to you."

Just then, the rain began, falling lightly at first, then with growing force. Trace appeared at Bridget's side just as she got a halter on Sis and fastened it. He was leading the stallion. "Is there a place we can take them?" he yelled over the roar of the rain.

The animals, overheated just moments before, were soaked.

Bridget thought of the old Indian lodge across the creek and pointed with one hand. "Over there!" she shouted back. The downpour had, at least, extinguished the flaming pine tree. "Back behind those trees. I'll show you!"

Trace caught her arm. "No," he told her. "The creek will be running pretty fast. You go inside!"

She shook her head. "These are my horses," she said stubbornly.

Trace threw up his free hand in a flash of frustration, but he let her lead the way to the creek, where she hiked her nightdress and wrapper up to her knees and tied them into a knot. The stream was indeed swollen, and between bolts of lightning, the surrounding countryside was darker than dark. Twice, while they were crossing, each of them leading a half-panicked horse, blue-gold light danced across the opposite bank.

It would have been a beautiful thing to see, Bridget thought, if it hadn't come so close to the water. The creek was without question the worst place they could possibly be in such weather, and the trees they were headed toward were the second worst.

The lodge had a hide roof and sturdy walls, though. When she and Skye and Noah had arrived at Primrose Creek in their ox-drawn wagon, she had considered taking the place for their home. In the end, she'd chosen the cabin because it had stone walls and was closer to the creek.

Bridget's feet and legs were numb by the time they got to the other side, and her shoes were probably ruined. The rain came down in torrents, making a sound on the water that might have been mistaken for the roar of a raging fire. They made their slippery way up the hillside and finally, finally, found the lodge itself.

Trace tied the stallion at one end of the long structure and then secured Sis at the other, while Bridget groped for something they could use to wipe down the horses. Being careful not to think too much about rats and spiders and other creatures that might take refuge in such places,

Bridget picked up a length of what felt like leather—no doubt it was part of the roof—and used that to dry the shivering mare as best she could. When she'd finished, she found her way to Trace, gave him the hide, and waited while he attended to the stallion.

Neither Bridget nor Trace spoke at all—they were both too spent to make idle conversation—until they were standing face to face, visible to each other only because of intermittent explosions of lightning. When he put his hands on her shoulders, pulled her close, and lowered his mouth to hers, it seemed perfectly natural.

Bridget was fairly certain her eyes were closed, and yet it seemed to her that the whole world burst into flames in the space of that kiss. A bolt of lightning coursed through her, delving deep into the earth, like roots of fire, shooting out through the top of her head like the tail of a rocket. She was dazed when Trace drew back; she swayed slightly, and he steadied her.

"We'd better get back," he said.

Bridget couldn't speak at all. She let him take her hand, though, and lead her out of the lodge, down the bank, across water that blazed with reflected lightning. She stumbled once, in the middle of the creek, went clear under, and came up laughing. She couldn't get any wetter than she already was.

Lamplight glowed from the cabin doorway; they followed it, Trace setting Bridget over the threshold before stepping inside himself, fastening the door behind him.

"Good thing you got the roof done," Skye said.

Bridget and Trace looked at each other, dripping wet, and laughed like a pair of fools.

"Look at you," Skye went on, all but shaking her finger. "You'll be down with pneumonia before morning if we don't do something."

Bridget was, all of a sudden, at a loss for what to do. It seemed she'd spent all her wits on getting the horses in out of the storm. Trace appeared to be equally bewildered; his lips—had he truly kissed her?—had turned blue, and his teeth were chattering.

Fortunately, Skye was more than ready to take charge. "Trace, you stay here by the stove, and I'll get you a blanket to wrap up in. You'll want to get out of those clothes first, of course." She took Bridget's arm. "I've laid out a dry nightgown for you and a towel for drying your hair." Then, sternly, "Trace, you keep your back turned."

He made a sound that might have been a groan or a raw-throated laugh. "Where's that whiskey?" he asked.

A few minutes later, when Trace had stripped and wrapped himself in one of several old quilts they'd brought from the farm, and she had gotten into her thickest flannel nightdress, they sat side by side in front of the inadequate little stove, sipping coffee laced with molasses and strong whiskey. Skye was there, alternately brushing and toweling

Bridget's long hair, so neither of them raised the subject of the kiss stolen in the dark ruin across the creek.

Bridget wasn't sure she could have brought the subject up, anyhow. She felt strangely shy, as though that kiss had been her first ever. As though it had been not just a kiss but an introduction to the fullness of womanhood, complete in itself. Never, not once, had Mitch's kisses affected her that way—but it was better not to follow such thoughts.

"Are we still going to town tomorrow?" Noah wanted to know.

Trace chuckled. "If the rain lets up," he said, "I suppose we'll go ahead."

Noah turned his hazel eyes to Bridget. "You'll come, too, won't you, Mama?" He looked so hopeful. And so like Mitch.

She reached out, laid her hand on his silky hair. "Yes, sweetheart. I'll go, too. Now, hadn't you better get back in bed? If you don't get your rest, you might be too tired to make a trip to town."

Noah nodded in eager agreement, leaned forward, and gave Bridget a good-night smack on the cheek.

Out of the corner of her eye, she saw Trace's crooked smile. "That was pretty sly," he murmured, when Skye was busy settling Noah down for what remained of the night.

She merely smiled and took another sip of the medicinal coffee.

Trace ran a hand through his hair and gazed at

the stove. "I'll get started on the barn as soon as I can," he said. "In the meantime, we'll use the place over there. I'll nail up the tarp to reinforce that roof."

She didn't want him to talk about roofs and barns and canvas tarps. She wanted him to explain how he'd had the audacity to kiss her that way, and why it had changed her forever. She laid a hand on his arm, the one covered by the soft fabric of the old quilt. "Trace?"

He met her gaze, waited.

And Skye came back, clucking like a mother hen trying to herd scattered chicks back to the nest. "Really, Bridget. You have so much hair—it'll be a *week* before it's dry."

Trace and Bridget were still staring at each other, in stricken silence now, and Bridget was certain her own expression must be as thunderstruck as Trace's.

Chapter

6

When he finally stretched out on the pallet of quilts and blankets Skye had made for him in front of the stove, Trace didn't expect to sleep. His clothes, draped over the edge of the spool table, would surely be dry by morning, and, thanks to the whiskey, the aching chill of wind and rain and creek water had left his flesh. No, it was the memory of the kiss he'd stolen from Bridget that would keep him awake; he could feel the heat of it lingering on his mouth, and the force of the emotions raised by her response still reverberated through his very bones.

He stared up at the underside of the roof he'd finished none too soon, listening to the soft patter of the rain, and wished that Bridget were there beside him, his to hold. He closed his eyes with a sigh, and in the next instant, he was asleep and dreaming. The confounding thing was that he knew he was actually lying on the floor of a cabin in the high country of Nevada, but his mind and spirit had strayed back to an earlier time in his life, and he could do nothing else but follow.

Mitch was up ahead, mounted on the fine black gelding Gideon had given him only a few months before, leading a charge across some swift and nameless river, sword raised and gleaming in the midday sun. Trace had fallen behind, some twenty minutes before, when his own spotted horse, also bred on the McQuarrys' farm, had picked up a stone and turned up lame.

By the time Trace had removed the stone and caught up with the other troops, Mitch was almost out of sight. Trace stood in the stirrups, just in time to see the gelding catch a sniper's bullet square in the side of its neck. The animal shrieked in terror and pain and flailed wildly, while Mitch tried in vain to control it. A crimson foam churned atop the water, and more shots were fired.

In the chaos that followed, Mitch somehow lost his seat in the saddle, disappeared under the water. Trace, oblivious to the shower of Rebel bullets pocking the surface of the river, struggled to reach his friend. The spotted mare balked, and there were other men shot, other horses as well, blocking the way.

Then, at last, he reached the drowning gelding, dove beneath the surface of the water, found Mitch floating motionless, eyes wide open, arms spread as if to receive his fate. His right foot had slipped through the stirrup, and he hadn't been able to pull free before he ran out of air.

Trace drew his knife, severed the stirrup from the saddle, and hauled Mitch to the surface.

The shooting had stopped, but Trace barely noticed. He dragged his best friend out of the river, laid him face down on the bank, and bore down on his back with both hands in an effort to force the water from Mitch's lungs. He was aware of a dull throbbing in his right thigh, but it would be some time before he realized he'd been wounded.

The barrel of a rifle prodded his shoulder; he looked up to see a young Reb standing over him, scared half to death but determined to do his duty. "He's dead, mister. And you're a prisoner now, so get to your feet if you can."

Trace wrenched Mitch over onto his back, yelled at him to blink or get up or just breathe. By then, though, Mitch's lips had turned a blue-gray color, and his eyes were empty. Trace swallowed a scream of protest and pain, swayed to his feet, and hoisted his friend off the ground, carrying him over one shoulder.

"You got to leave him here, Yank," the boy persisted. He couldn't have been more than sixteen, that kid in the ill-fitting gray woolen jacket; he still had spots on his face.

Trace glared at his unlikely captor. "I mean to bury him," he said. "If you want to stop me, you'd best just shoot me right here."

The boy's gaze dropped to Trace's bloody leg. "Looks like somebody already done that," he said, without triumph. He prodded Trace with the rifle barrel again, but cautiously. "They ain't gonna let you bury him. There's too many others that need burying."

Trace gripped the rifle barrel and forced it aside, twisting it out of the boy's grasp in the process. It clattered to the wet, smooth pebbles on the river-bank, where it lay, unclaimed. "You wave that thing in my face again," he said fiercely, "and I'm going to jam it in one end of you and out the other." Then he started up the slope to the grassy meadow above, and the Confederates made way for him to pass.

Someone brought him a shovel; he began to dig the grave. He was in a strange state of mind, half outside himself, a step behind, like his own hapless ghost. He thought he might have gone wild with the force of his grief, if only he could catch up to himself.

They let him dig and dig, those Rebs, and at some point, a couple of them joined in. When the hole was deep enough, Trace wrapped Mitch's body in a blanket someone had brought, got down into the grave himself and lay his lifeless friend at his feet as gently as if he'd been a sleeping baby.

"Good-bye," he said, and then his knees gave way, and his mind went dark, one shadow at a time.

"Trace?" A hand rested firmly on his shoulder, gave him a shake. "Trace, wake up. You're dream-ing."

He opened his eyes and looked up to see Bridget

bending over him, hair trailing to her waist. "I'm sorry," he murmured, and made to sit up. She stepped back so he could.

She sat down on one of the crate chairs, her hands folded in her lap. The rain had stopped, and the moon must have come out, too, because no lamps were burning, and he could see her so plainly, in her white flannel nightdress. "You were calling to Mitch," she said, very softly.

He sighed, shoved a hand through his hair. For some reason, he couldn't look at her. "Yeah," he said. "I didn't mean to wake you."

"You didn't," she replied. "I was thinking about—about tonight."

The kiss. He would have preferred to talk about Mitch. "I shouldn't have done that."

"No, you shouldn't have," she agreed readily. "And I shouldn't have responded the way I did. It's just that—it's just that I've been so lonely."

"I know," he said. "I know."

She straightened her spine a little. "Do you suppose the horses are all right?"

He grinned, relieved at the change of subject, though a part of him was mighty disappointed that she could dismiss a kiss like that one so easily. "They're in out of the rain. For tonight, that's enough."

She smiled a small, wobbly smile. "Thank you, Trace. I don't know what I would have done if you hadn't been here—the tarp would never have kept out a storm like that, and heaven only knows what would have happened to Sis and the stallion."

He wanted to touch her cheek, her hand, her shoulder, but he didn't dare. He'd stepped out of line as it was, kissing her the way he had, and he was cold again, as cold as if he'd really been in that bloody river so far away, trying desperately, hopelessly, to save his best friend.

"Go back to bed, Bridget," he said hoarsely.

She hesitated, then rose, put more wood into the stove, and watched him for a long time in pensive silence. Finally, she spoke. "Did he suffer? Mitch, I mean?"

Trace bit his lower lip, held her gaze. "I don't think so," he said. "There was a gash in the back of his head. He must have struck it on a rock when he was thrown."

"You did everything you could, Trace," she whispered. "I know you did."

It came upon him suddenly sometimes, took him by surprise even in the broad light of day, the knowledge that Mitch was dead, that he'd never see him again. After the dream, though, the grief was worse, as fresh as if the incident had happened only hours ago, instead of years. "That's kind of you, Mrs. McQuarry," he said, and wondered at the edge in his voice even as he spoke, "considering your stated opinion that I'm to blame for what happened." In truth, he blamed himself. And he was beginning to suspect that he hadn't come to Primrose Creek set on marrying Bridget because of any promise to Mitch but for reasons of his own. Selfish ones.

She paled; he saw that in the dim light, hated himself for it. And then she said something he'd never have expected to hear her say. "I was wrong, Trace. I'm sorry. Mitch was a man, not a little boy, and he wouldn't have gone to war if he hadn't wanted to."

There was nothing he could say to that. It was wholly true. Though amiable and maybe even naive, Mitch had been eager for adventure. He'd have joined the fighting even if Trace had refused to go along; it was just that neither of them had really expected to die. They'd been so young, with their blood pulsing in their veins, convinced they would go home triumphant one day, together, and tell stories about their experiences until they were both too old to rightly recall any of it.

Only it hadn't happened that way.

Trace lay down. The dirt floor was hard, even wrapped in quilts the way he was, and the cold seemed to seep through his skin.

"First thing, after I get the barn built," he said, turning away from Bridget and dragging the covers up to his ear, "I mean to put a bedroom on the back of this cabin. You and I aren't sleeping out here once we're married." He waited for her protest, but she said nothing at all. He heard her cross the room, get back into bed, and sigh.

When Bridget awakened the next morning, with burning eyes and an irritating stuffiness in her nose, Trace had already left the house. She was fairly certain he'd gone to fetch the horses back from the lodge across the creek, and a glance out the front window confirmed the fact. He was leading Sis by her halter, while Windfall followed amenably.

The air was golden, scrubbed clean by last night's storm, and the creek was a ribbon of bright silver, light in motion. It was only then, watching the man and the two horses coming up the near bank, that she realized why the stallion obeyed Trace so readily.

She went outside and watched, arms folded loosely in front of her, while Trace put both Sis and the stallion out to graze, each tethered to a separate line.

"What's his true name?" she asked, when Trace finally came to stand before her, looking like a Norse god in the dazzling glow of the morning sun. "The stallion, I mean."

Trace watched her solemnly for a few moments, then he flashed that illegal grin. "I call him Sentinel," he said.

She set her hands on her hips and tried to be annoyed, but she just couldn't manage it. Not on such a beautiful day. "Why didn't you tell me he was yours in the first place?"

He scratched the back of his head, narrowed his eyes to a good-natured squint. "That would have been one less reason to stay here," he said, "and I do mean to stay. Besides, I reckoned you'd figure it out on your own sooner or later, given that I showed up here on foot, carrying my saddle. Those Paiutes jumped me, one fine morning before I'd had my coffee, and relieved me of the horse. Evidently, they couldn't handle him and decided to pass the problem on to you." He stopped smiling. "The thing that troubles me about that is, it means they were watching this place. I'd be willing to bet they knew you and Skye and the boy were here alone, and they sure as hell had their eye on those oxen for a while, too."

Bridget had imagined the Indians watching her and Skye as they went about their chores, watching Noah, but until now, she'd never allowed herself to entertain the thought for too long. It was too frightening. "If that's so, then by now they know you're here."

He scanned the surrounding countryside, as though he expected the pack of renegades to come shrieking out of the timber, mounted on their war ponies and waving tomahawks over their heads. "Maybe it's just that I didn't get much rest last night," he said, "but I've got a real uneasy feeling just now. You keep Skye and Noah close by until it's time to leave for town."

Bridget nodded, unconsciously wringing the fabric of her skirt with both hands. "You'd best move your things into the cabin," she said.

"I'll do that," he replied.

As he walked away to gather up his rain-soaked belongings, Bridget harbored the notion that he might have been trying to scare her so she would let him stay inside the house. Instantly, she dismissed the idea. Trace was certainly no model of decorum, but he'd never use fear to get what he wanted. Anyway, the small hairs on her nape were standing up.

They left for Primrose Creek an hour later, Skye and Noah riding bareback on Sis, Trace on the stallion, with Bridget side-saddle in front of him. She tried to ignore the way it made her feel, having Trace's arms around her that way, however loosely, but the effort proved useless. Ever since he'd kissed her the night before—and honesty compelled her to consider the fact that she had most definitely kissed him back—she'd had a strange, boneless feeling, as though some slow, sweet fever had taken root inside her, causing her to melt away, digit by digit, limb by limb.

It was an exceedingly peculiar sensation, one she had never experienced before, even in her most intimate moments with Mitch. There had been few enough of those, of course, since her bridegroom had gone away to war barely a week after their wedding, leaving her pregnant with a child he would never see.

She had been filled with tenderness for Mitch. With Trace, it was something else entirely—a deep and violent yearning to touch him, to surrender to him, to lie beneath him. But there was the fury, too—always the fury. Where had he been when the world was crumbling around her, when the farm was overrun with carpetbaggers and

Granddaddy was dying and she'd needed his help? Where?

Heat thrummed in her face, and she was glad her back was turned to him, because he would have seen too much if he'd been able to look at her straight on.

Water dappled the mud-and-manure streets of Primrose Creek, standing in dirty puddles big as lakes. The tents all had a sodden look about them, their tops weighted and dripping, but the towns-people seemed exuberant, and Bridget thought she understood their cheerful mood. There was some-thing about a storm like last night's that made a person feel as though the world had been washed and polished, groomed for a new start.

Jake Vigil's grand mansion was at the far end of town, and the sawmill was beyond, just a long log structure, really, with a crudely lettered sign on the roof announcing lumber for sale. Jake himself was a tower of a man, standing well over six feet, broad-shouldered and square-jawed, with thoughtful hazel eyes and a head full of curly brown hair. Handsome as he was, Mr. Vigil was shy, at least around anyone in a skirt. Just seeing Bridget and Skye made him flush crimson and look away quickly, as if he'd found them somehow, well, indisposed.

Trace dismounted and introduced himself. He and Vigil shook hands, and then they vanished inside the mill building, deep in discussion.

Bridget took that opportunity to look around for

a bank. Most likely, she wouldn't be able to get a loan anyhow, especially now that she wouldn't have the stallion for collateral, but she had to do something. Granddaddy had meant the Primrose Creek tract to stay in the family, her share and Skye's, and Christy and Megan's, too.

"What are you looking for?" Skye asked, always curious.

"A bank," Bridget said. "I thought if—"

"You thought if you borrowed money and paid Christy and Megan for their land, they'd never have cause to come out here and live across the creek from us."

Bridget was affronted, though not, if the truth were known, precisely justified in her response. She did cherish a certain secret worry that their cousins would come to Primrose Creek to claim their inheritance, unlikely as it seemed. The old feud would surely start up again. "You can't seriously think they'll *ever* set foot in a place like this," she said, as much to convince herself as Skye. Her conscience was troubling her a little, for she knew full well that Gideon hadn't meant for Christy and Megan to sell their land. He might even have put something in his will that would prevent it.

"They don't truly belong in England," Skye said. "The farm was home to them, just like it was to us. But now that's gone, and *this* is home."

Bridget rolled her eyes. "Can you really picture those two here, mincing down the street in their satin slippers, pressing their linen handkerchiefs to their pert little noses?" She was convinced she was safe in making the obvious assumption, for she truly couldn't imagine Christy and Megan in these surroundings.

Skye looked obstinate. "They'll come to Primrose Creek, Bridget. Just you wait and see. And you'd better be nice to them, too."

Before Bridget was forced to offer a reply, she spotted a sign hanging outside an especially ragged tent just down the road. *Preaching, this Sunday,* it read. Well, if there wasn't a bank, at least there was a church of sorts. The mining town might have stumbled unwittingly into the path of civilization after all.

Trace came out of the mill, notable for its lack of a shrieking saw if nothing else, looking very pleased with himself.

"We'll have a barn in no time at all," he said, "and a bedroom right after that."

Skye looked from Trace to Bridget, blushed a little, and then smiled. "You're adding a room?"

Trace nodded, as though there were nothing unusual or improper about discussing such accommodations in front of a young girl and a child. Not to mention his best friend's widow. "Come next spring," he said easily, "I'll build one for you, too, little sister, and one for Noah here."

Skye beamed at the prospect, then lapsed into a frown. "I'll be almost seventeen then. Ready to marry up with somebody and have my own place, next to Bridget's."

He chuckled. "Don't be in such a hurry, monkey," he said. "You'll be a long time married, after all."

Bridget glanced away. Her face felt hot again. "Is there a bank in this town?" she asked, maybe with just a hint of testiness in her voice.

"Now, Mrs. McQuarry," Trace drawled, pushing his hat to the back of his head and looking up at her with eyes full of mischief, "what in all the blue-skied world would you want with such an institution as that?"

She stiffened. She hated it when he called her "Mrs. McQuarry" in that particular tone, as though she were a young girl playing house and serving make-believe tea in miniature cups, instead of a woman grown, with a child to raise. "That ought to be perfectly obvious, *Mr. Qualtrough.* I want to borrow a sum of money and buy the land across the creek before our cousins sell it to someone—er—undesirable."

He was holding the cheek piece of the stallion's bridle, his shoulder touching Bridget's right knee and part of her thigh. She wished he wouldn't stand so close; it made her feel as if she were caught in the middle of the creek, with lightning striking all around her. "Gideon meant that land for Christy and Megan. I reckon you ought to leave them to decide what to do with it."

Bridget set her jaw, released it with an effort. "Christy asked me to buy the land," she said. "Read the letter if you don't believe me."

"Oh, I believe you, all right," Trace said, tugging the brim of his hat forward a little so it shaded his eyes. "But I figure you'd better just wait and see what happens before you go taking on any debts. You know Christy's impetuous; she might have changed her mind by now, and Megan would have had a thing or two to say about it, too, since half that tract is hers."

There was no sense in arguing, especially when Skye was right there, listening in, ready to take Trace's side in the matter. "It would appear that there is a church here," she said, because the silence had stretched to an uncomfortable length.

"Good," Trace said, grinning again. "We can get married proper-like."

"I have no intention of marrying you," Bridget informed him, out of pique and habit.

He just looked at her, with the memory of that kiss laughing in his eyes. His expression said, *Think what you like*. And he took the stallion's reins in one hand and headed for the tent in question.

"We'd like to get married," Trace said, when a white-haired man came out of the church tent, smiling at the prospect of welcoming stray sheep into the fold.

The reverend looked at Skye, then at Bridget, obviously puzzled.

"This one," Trace told him helpfully, laying a hand on Bridget's thigh, big as life, right there in front of God and everybody. He was just lucky she didn't have a riding quirt in her hand. "I figure we ought to get the words said as soon as possible, on account of we're living in sin."

Bridget's mouth dropped open. Skye giggled behind one hand, while Noah reached out both arms for Trace and said, "Papa, papa."

Trace took the boy from the saddle and settled him on one of his shoulders. The reverend took a handkerchief from the pocket of his frayed black waistcoat and wiped his brow.

"You can see," Trace added in a confidential tone, "that it's urgent."

"Yes, indeed," said the reverend. "Yes, indeed. Well, come inside, all of you, and let's attend to this matter."

"Now, wait just one moment," Bridget protested. "I ought to have something to say about this, it seems to me, and I—"

Skye and Trace and Noah all turned their gazes in her direction at once. She thought of unfriendly Indians and thunderstorms, snakebites and starvation, and knew in that moment that she *had* to agree to the marriage if she were going to live in the same skin with her conscience.

"All right," she said. "All right. But I would like a word with my future husband before the ceremony. *Alone.*"

Beaming, Skye sprang down from Sis's back, tied her to the nearest hitching post, and, collecting Noah from Trace's shoulders, followed the reverend into the church tent.

Trace put his hands on Bridget's waist and lifted

her down, and just that much contact took her
breath away, so that it was a moment or two before
she could speak.

"Now, you listen to me, Trace Qualtrough," she
whispered in a burst, waggling a finger under his
nose. "We might be man and wife after this, but
that does *not* mean that you will—that I will allow
you to—"

He chuckled, bent to place a light, teasing kiss
on her mouth, effectively silencing her. "I understand," he said. "We'll wait until you're ready or
until that bedroom is finished, whichever comes
first."

Bridget's mouth opened again; he closed it with
a slight upward pressure from the fingertips of his
right hand.

"This isn't a game, Bridget. I want a real wife. A
home. Children."

She swallowed. "Children?" She hadn't thought
much about that since Mitch was killed, though
she'd wanted a big family before he died, for she
hadn't expected to marry again.

"A whole passel of them," he said.

"Good heavens," Bridget said, and fanned her
face with one hand.

He laughed again, took her arm, and propelled
her toward the doorway of the church tent. "Now,
don't go fretting yourself," he teased in an under-
tone. "I'll wait as long as a week."

It happened in a whirl of small events that all fit
together to seal Bridget's fate, once and for all. The

pastor of Primrose Creek's first church introduced himself as "Reverend Taylor, just Taylor." There were rows of benches, and someone had erected a modest pulpit of raw, unpainted wood.

Skye stood at Bridget's side, to serve as her maid of honor, and Noah, settled comfortably on Trace's hip, was the best man. The reverend cleared his throat and opened his prayer book with a solemnity suitable for such an occasion.

Bridget thought of running, just turning on her heel and fleeing, more than once, but the ceremony was over before she'd gotten up the nerve. Reverend Taylor pronounced her and Trace husband and wife, and Trace leaned down and touched his mouth to Bridget's.

The powerful, heated shock of that second kiss turned her already riotous senses to an indescribable muddle of wildly varying sensations. She had never guessed that a simple peck on the lips could provoke such havoc; this was very different from the quiet tenderness she'd felt when Mitch kissed her. Very different indeed.

She looked down at the golden band Trace had slipped onto her left-hand ring finger and was amazed. Trace had showed her that ring only a few days before and told her with certainty that they were about to be married. She hadn't believed him, but here she was, with a husband and a new name. She'd make an entry in the McQuarry Bible as soon as she got home.

After the wedding, Trace bought dinner for the

four of them in the mess tent next to Jake Vigil's sawmill, surrounded by lumbermen and miners, drifters and farmers. Bridget thought they must all know she'd gone ahead and married Trace Qualtrough even though she'd sworn she could not be persuaded. The food, venison stew and fresh bread with lots of butter, was delicious, but Bridget didn't eat much. She was thinking about the coming night, her wedding night, wondering if Trace would honor his promise to wait until she was ready.

Even in her agitated state, Bridget noticed the way the men crowding the tent kept stealing sidelong glances at Skye, and that brought all her protective instincts to the fore. Very likely, these men knew Trace had been staying at the cabin and had concluded that the McQuarry women must be loose.

It ought to be obvious to these men that Skye was far too young and too innocent for courting, but even if they had noticed, they did not seem to be dissuaded. One of them, a young man in workman's clothes, had the nerve to approach the table. He had dark hair and green eyes, and Bridget supposed he was handsome enough, but he didn't look as though he had good prospects.

He cleared his throat and reddened a little when Skye looked up at him and smiled questioningly. The onlookers—and that included virtually everyone else in the mess tent—hooted and elbowed one another.

"My name's Tom Barkley," the boy said.

Skye glanced at Bridget, then met Barkley's green gaze. "Skye McQuarry."

More hoots and howls. Tom turned and took in the whole place with an angry gesture of one hand—the hand that held his slouch hat. "You all tend to your own business," he said, "and I'll tend to mine."

"Do something," Bridget whispered, elbowing Trace.

He reached for another piece of bread and buttered it calmly. "About what?" he asked, though he knew perfectly well.

"There's a dance on Saturday night," Tom said to Skye. "I would count it an honor if you'd let me bring you."

Bridget opened her mouth, fell silent when Trace's hand came to rest lightly on her forearm.

Skye averted her gaze for a few moments, then looked up into Tom's earnest, youthful face and nodded. "I'd like that," she said.

A great tension seemed to leave Tom at her agreement; his serious expression turned to a smile that even Bridget would have had to admit was endearing. If anyone would have asked her, that is. Nobody did.

"I'll come by for you at six o'clock," Tom Barkley said.

Skye regarded him steadily. "I—I don't really know how to dance."

Tom's grin broadened. "That's all right," he said

generously. "Neither do I. I reckon we can work it out together."

Bridget cast a quick, sidelong glance in her husband's direction.

"Your baby sister is old enough to have callers," he said very quietly. "Loosen your grip, if you don't want to drive her off."

Bridget sighed, folded her hands in her lap, and waited for the meal to end. All she wanted now was to go home, push up her sleeves, and deal with whatever was going to happen next.

Chapter

7

*T*race acted as if nothing much had happened when they got home; without a word about the wedding, he put the horses to pasture and proceeded to pace off the area of the barn, pounding stakes into the ground to mark the corners. Bridget stood watching him until he looked her way and waved, and then she turned on one heel and fled into the cabin.

Noah was sitting on the floor, playing with the top Trace had bought for him, and Skye was on her knees in front of the trunk, pawing through the assorted garments inside.

"That blue silk," she said in a distracted tone of voice. "You brought that, didn't you? You didn't leave it behind in Virginia?"

Bridget felt a pang of nostalgia. Trace was right; Skye was no longer a little girl, and it was natural for her to have suitors. Knowing those things did nothing to ease Bridget's aching heart, however.

She had been as much a mother to Skye as an elder sister, and she loved her with a fierce intensity. "It's there somewhere," she said.

Skye found the gown, held it up by the shoulders. "It ought to fit, if I let it out a little and take down the hem." She met Bridget's gaze at last, clutching the simple dress against her chest as though it were woven of golden thread and trimmed in pearls. "I can wear it, can't I? Please?"

Bridget swallowed. She cared nothing about the dress, but her sister's well-being was another matter. "Yes," she said. "You can wear it. But don't you think—well—shouldn't you get to know Mr. Barkley a little better, before you go off to a dance with him?"

Skye's lovely face darkened. She got to her feet, holding the gown carefully the whole time. "How can I get to know the man at all if I can't talk to him?" she countered. She had an obstinate glint in her eyes, and her chin jutted out a little way. "I'm going to that dance, even if you won't let me borrow this dress."

"It's yours," Bridget said gently. Things would change between Skye and herself, after this day. There would be more callers, more dances, more dangers than a girl of sixteen could imagine. All the same, Skye would need her sister less and less, from now on, until finally she wouldn't need her at all.

The thought made a lonely ache in Bridget's chest. Trace was right; she had to let go of Skye, but it was one of the hardest things she'd ever had to do. Even worse, it wouldn't be long before Noah, too, was grown.

Skye must have seen something in the expression on Bridget's face, for she sighed, crossed the room, and embraced her quickly but with real affection. "You've always protected me, looked after me, worried about me," she said, tears glistening at the roots of her lashes. "I'll always be grateful. But don't you see, Bridge? It's your turn to be happy. For once in your life, think of yourself."

Bridget sniffled, summoned up a wavery smile. "I'm married," she said. "Oh, Skye, what on earth possessed me to take Trace Qualtrough for a husband?"

Skye laughed and kissed Bridget's forehead. "I think you showed a great deal of discernment, choosing him. It surprised me a little, to tell the truth—I was afraid you'd either never marry again or hitch yourself to somebody who wanted taking care of." She paused, blushing a little when she saw Bridget's face quicken with amused interest. "You know, because you're so strong and everything. Let him love you, Bridge. Please, just set your pride aside and let Trace love you."

Bridget was forced to turn away then. Love had nothing to do with her marriage to Trace; she'd loved one man in her life, and that was Mitch. To let those feelings die would be a cruelty, an unthinkable betrayal. No, her union with Trace was merely one of convenience. "You'd best get started on that dress," she said, tying on an apron, "if you expect to have it ready by Saturday."

Skye let out a long sigh.

Noah had gone to the doorway, where the afternoon sun shone around him. "Listen, Mama. There's wagons coming."

Sure enough, the faint sound of creaking wheels and horses' hooves found its way across the creek. "That would be the lumber Trace ordered for the barn," Bridget said. *And the bedroom,* added a voice in her mind.

How long, she wondered, without examining her reasons too closely, did it take to build a barn?

To Skye's delight, Tom Barkley was driving one of the two huge wagons; he and Mr. Vigil drove right across the creek without even pausing, calling to their reluctant teams and slapping down the reins.

"Tom here had himself an idea," Mr. Vigil said, cocking a thumb in the other man's direction, when Bridget joined the visitors and her husband—*her husband*—on the future site of the barn. "Said we ought to have the Saturday night dance out here, at your place. Some of us could come early and help you raise the walls." He looked up, assessed the sky. "Sooner you have shelter for your stock, the better. The weather can change pretty quickly around here. Turn nasty, the way it did last night."

Bridget gnawed on her lower lip. A barn could go up pretty quickly when folks lent a hand, and that meant she might find herself sharing a room with Trace far sooner than she'd expected. An unseemly thrill raced through her, chased by a sense of delicious alarm. She didn't dare glance in Trace's direction, because she knew he'd be looking at her, reading her mind. Grinning.

"We'd be obliged for any help," she heard Trace say.

It was settled, as easily as that. Trace and Mr. Vigil and Tom set themselves to unloading the lumber and two kegs of nails, and then the visitors took their leave, rattling away in their huge, empty wagons.

Stacks of fragrant timber stood all around.

"I suppose you think you're pretty clever," Bridget said to Trace under her breath as the two of them stood side by side, waving Tom and Jake Vigil out of sight. "You'll have that barn finished in a fraction of the time with so much help. And how did you pay for all this?"

Trace laughed. "I can't figure out whether you're pleased or ready to tie into me with your claws out. As for the lumber, I made a swap with Jake. His pinewood for my help finishing his mill."

"You amaze me," Bridget confessed.

And Trace laughed again. "Just you wait," he said. "There are more surprises ahead."

Saturday morning brought seventeen men, armed with saws and hammers, chisels and measuring sticks. The barn seemed to take shape before

Bridget's very eyes; every time she ventured to peer around the corner of the cabin, another wall was framed. By late afternoon, the walls were up, and the roof was being nailed into place.

Skye changed into her carefully altered dancing gown well beforehand, put her hair up, let it down, put it up again. She paced and waited and watched the progress of the sun as it descended in the western skies, as if by watching she could hurry it along. Bridget hid her smile and concentrated on keeping track of Noah; he wanted very much to participate in the barn building, but he was forbidden to go near the project. Even Trace had agreed to that; it was simply too dangerous.

Skye was visibly relieved when sunset finally settled over the land, and Bridget herself felt a certain sweet excitement. Now, the horses would have stalls, walls to keep out wolves and at least discourage unfriendly Indians, a thick roof to shelter them from rain and wind and snow. She could get a cow. Plant a field of hay next summer. . . .

But it wasn't the practicality of having a barn that made her want to sing, and she knew it. It was the idea of dancing with Trace, being held in his arms, looking up into his eyes. She'd hardly thought of anything else since their wedding three days before, even though Trace had been nothing if not a gentleman. He hadn't even tried to kiss her, as a matter of fact.

She wasn't sure how she felt about that. On the one hand, she'd have been furious if he made any untoward advances. On the other, she was indignant that he *hadn't*.

As evening approached, guests began to arrive, in wagons, in buggies, on foot, and on horseback. Lanterns were lit, and the musicians—miners with fiddles and a dark-skinned man with a guitar—set themselves up to play in the pitch-scented confines of the new barn. There were a few women, grim-faced and clearly on the lookout for sin run amok, but most of the revelers were men. When the music started, a spirited jig, they danced with one another. Skye and Mr. Barkley joined in, laughing at their own stumbling efforts to get in step, and Bridget looked on, clapping in time to the music, Noah at her side.

Trace came up behind her, mussed Noah's hair with one hand.

"Well, Mrs. Qualtrough," Trace said. "What do you think of your barn?"

Mrs. Qualtrough. Now, wasn't that something? A sweet quiver started in the pit of her stomach and radiated outward, into every part of her. "It's very sturdy," she allowed.

He grinned. "That it is," he said. "Plenty of lumber left, too. I can start building on to the house right away."

Bridget knew he was trying to get a rise out of her, and she was darned if she'd let him succeed. He'd shaken her up enough as it was.

It was about time somebody turned the tables on Trace Qualtrough. "Yes," she said, watching the dancers, clapping her hands, smiling. "And I've been thinking. You're doing all the work. You ought to have that room to yourself."

He took her elbow, turned her to face him, and pulled her into his arms. Noah was already at the other end of the barn by that time—the older he got, the faster he moved, it seemed to Bridget—watching the fiddlers ply their bows, and a dizzy feeling made her head light. The musicians took up a reel, and Trace spun both of them into its midst without missing a step.

"That wasn't our agreement," he pointed out.

Bridget beamed up at him, but the familiar anger, never far from the surface, was crackling inside her. "Are you saying that I must pay for this barn with my favors?"

He wasn't even pretending to smile by then, but he kept up with the lively tune spilling from the fiddles and the guitar, and made Bridget keep up, too. "You know damn well that isn't what I meant," he said. "You're my wife. I told you, I want a real marriage—complete with kids."

"What about Mitch?"

He stopped, pulled her out of the barn to stand with him under a drapery of sparkling stars. "Mitch," he said, his face close to hers, "is dead. It's about time you accepted that."

Bridget wanted to slug him, because deep down, she knew he was right, and it was too painful a thing to admit. "Do you think I need reminding of that? He's lying in the ground somewhere, while we're—we're—" She gestured toward the barn, spilling light and music. *"Dancing."*

He took her by the sides of her waist and dragged her hard against him. "What's wrong with that, Bridget?" he demanded. "Husbands and wives dance together."

She was breathless. He was, well, hard. Everywhere. The warm summer night seemed even warmer, all of a sudden. She pulled away. "You didn't come home," she seethed, and suddenly tears were streaming down her face. "You wrote me a letter to tell me my husband was dead, but *you didn't come home*. Damn you, I watched the road for you, every day and every night—"

Trace stared at her, obviously shocked. "Is that what's got you riled?" he asked. "I was in a prison hospital, Bridget. I nearly lost my leg."

It was her turn to be stunned. "But you didn't mention that, in the letter—"

"Damn it, Bridget," Trace went on, "Mitch was my best friend, and losing him was probably the worst thing that ever happened to me. I was thinking about that, and besides, it was three months before I could bribe a Reb into posting that letter." He closed his eyes for a moment, and when he spoke again, his voice was lower, softer. "When are we going to let the past rest with Mitch and move on?"

Bridget swallowed; she was still reeling. "You were shot? Thrown into prison?"

"Yes," he snapped. He was holding her firmly by the upper arms, and she knew he wanted to shake her. She also knew he wouldn't. "And don't pretend you don't know I was in love with you. In case you've forgotten, I begged you not to marry Mitch."

She closed her eyes, remembering that interlude in her grandmother's fragrant garden. Absorbing the dual realization that she had indeed known how Trace felt, and that she'd denied it ever since. Moreover, she'd disavowed her own passions as well.

Trace went on, his words picking up steam as his temper rose. He was relentless. "And what's more, you loved me in return. You married Mitch because you thought you could keep him from going to war that way. You thought you could *save* him, Bridget, and that's a damn pitiful reason to marry anybody!"

Tears burned behind Bridget's eye sockets. "Stop it."

"I won't stop it," Trace said, holding her wrists now. "I loved you then, and I love you now, and I'm not about to let you cling to a dead man's coattails until it's too late. I'm through living out that lie, Bridget, and so are you!"

Shame filled her, for she could not refute what Trace had said. She had always cared for him. She always would. But she had sworn her loyalty to Mitch, she had borne his son, all the while loving another man. His best friend. It was that she had to make up for: the deception. Mitch had died believing she loved him.

Trace caught her face between his hands, leaned

in, and kissed her, hard. She melted, opened her mouth to him, opened her soul. Too soon, he set her away from him with a swiftness that was at once unwilling and resolute. His breathing was quick and ragged, and Bridget, with one palm resting against his chest, could feel his heart pounding. "Enough," he said. "Enough." He might have been speaking to himself, as well as to her. When he met her eyes, she was chilled by the sorrow she saw in his face. "I love you, and I want you. Oh, God, how I want you. But when you come to my bed, Bridget, you have to come alone. You can't bring Mitch with you."

The implication stung fiercely. She drew back her hand, ready to slap Trace hard across the face, but in the end, she couldn't make herself do it.

It was then, as they stood facing each other, their fractured dreams lying between them, that the raid began.

It started with a single, blood-chilling shriek, swelling out of the darkness like a gust of the devil's breath. In the next moment, Indians came from every direction, mounted on their shaggy, hungry ponies, spears and rifles in hand. Trace shouted a warning to the people in the barn—not that one was necessary—grabbed Bridget by the arm, and hurled her under the nearest wagon.

"Stay there!" he ordered.

Noah. Skye. Bridget went out the other side and raced toward the barn.

She heard the horse, felt the thunder rising up

out of the ground, reverberating through her lower limbs like an earthquake, and then a steel-hard arm encircled her waist, and she was dragged up onto the back of a horse. She tried to scream, but the sound lodged in her throat.

The Indian growled something at her in his own language, but Bridget understood, all the same. He was warning her to be silent, and when he pressed the blade of his knife to the side of her neck a second later, she knew he meant it.

Dazed, sick with horror, Bridget watched as the beautiful new barn went up in flames. *Noah!* She screamed inwardly. *Skye!*

Gunfire erupted all around them after that, and out of the corner of one eye, Bridget saw that the house was on fire as well. *Trace,* she pleaded silently, *Trace.*

Fear gnawed at Bridget's insides, brought a sticky sweat out all over her body. Crimson reflections danced off the flesh of Indians and horses, and there was so much noise, yelling and shooting. So much fire.

Bridget squinted, her eyes burning in the thickening smoke of her burning hopes, searching in vain for even a glimpse of her son, her sister, and Trace. Oh, God, where was Trace? Had they killed him, these marauding savages—not Paiutes, Bridget could see, but rogues and outlaws of many different tribes.

The man who held her prisoner tightened his grip and shouted something to the others. Then he spurred the pony hard with his heels, and they were jolting away, into the night. Into the terrifying unknown.

Bridget was numb where her own fate was concerned; she could not think beyond the terror that she would never see her family again. *Oh, God,* she prayed, *don't let them be dead. I can't bear to lose any of them.*

It seemed to Bridget that they rode endlessly, on and on, and at a teeth-clattering speed. Uphill, down again, through dark, gloomy trees, smelling incongruously of Christmas. Finally, toward dawn, they reached a camp of sorts, a smoky place, ripe with the smells of untanned animal hides, horses, and human beings.

When Bridget was flung to the ground, she scrambled immediately to her feet, running among the horses, searching desperately for her sister or her son. The renegades laughed at her efforts, and one of them put his foot out to make hard contact with her shoulder and send her sprawling.

She got up immediately and hurtled toward the offender, furious as a scalded cat. Like everyone else, she'd wondered, from time to time, if she were capable of killing. Now, she knew the answer.

She scrabbled halfway up the raider's leg, clawing her way toward his face.

He swore—she didn't need to know his language to recognize a curse—and kicked her again, this time harder. She struck the ground, felt a stone or a horse's hoof stab at her left temple, and lost consciousness.

"Mizz Qualtrough?" The voice was feminine, a cautious whisper. A moment passed before Bridget realized the other person was speaking English. "Mizz Qualtrough, are you all right?"

Bridget opened her eyes. Her headache pulsed through her entire body, in time with her runaway heartbeat, and she found that she was seated on the ground, tied at the wrists and ankles with painfully tight rawhide, the rough bark of a tree biting into her back. She wanted to throw up but somehow managed to control the impulse.

"Mizz Qualtrough?"

She peered at her fellow captive—Miss Florence Coffin, until then a member of the Primrose Creek faction who pretty much kept to themselves. Bridget had always considered them somewhat standoffish, but such things hardly mattered in their present circumstances.

Florence looked some the worse for wear, with her hair straggling and her dress torn, but her chin was up, and her eyes snapped with the determination to survive, no matter what.

"Miss Coffin," Bridget finally acknowledged, straining her neck to look around. "Are there others?"

"I don't think so," the other woman said. "And given the situation, I think you ought to call me Flossie."

Bridget smiled to herself, in spite of everything, because she had never once imagined this usually dour woman as a Flossie. Of course, she'd only seen her at a distance, and they'd never spoken. "My name is Bridget," she said.

"I know," replied Flossie with a sigh. "What do you suppose they mean to do with us?"

The possibilities didn't bear thinking about, but Bridget thought of them all the same, and bile rushed into the back of her throat, burning like acid. Again, she wanted to vomit; again, she stifled the impulse. "Let's concentrate on getting out of here," she said when she could manage to speak. "They probably mean to trade us for something. Horses, maybe, or food."

Flossie looked skeptical. She'd heard the same terrifying stories of slavery, rape, scalping, and all-over tattooing as Bridget had, no doubt, but she kept her spine straight. You had to admire a person with that much gumption. "Let's hope you're right."

"Did—did you see—was anyone killed?"

"I don't know," Flossie replied, and now her gaze was gentle. Why, Bridget wondered, had she ever imagined these townswomen, however distant, as anything other than ordinary human beings, trying to make their way in a difficult world? "Seems likely, with all that shooting, that somebody's got to be dead."

Bridget couldn't answer, and for a while, she and Flossie just sat there in silence, wrestling with their own thoughts. The birds began to chirp a morning song, and as light spilled across the camp, they saw that there were no tepees or lodges, just a campfire, a closely guarded band of some two dozen grazing horses, and about half that many Indians, all in various states of drunkenness. If there were other captives, they were somewhere out of sight.

Hatred spilled through Bridget's heart, cold and bracing. Her headache eased a little, and so did the nausea centered in her middle. If they'd harmed any of the people she loved, Skye and Noah and, yes, Trace, she'd see every one of these miscreants in hell, even if she had to lead them there by the hand, one by one.

As if discerning her thoughts, one of the men got up and staggered toward her, a foul grin creasing his filthy, painted face. Only then, in the light of day, did she see that the man was white, merely posing as an Indian. A quick glance around the camp confirmed that most of the others were, too.

Bridget was sure this particular scoundrel was the one who **had** kicked her to the ground, and she glared at him.

"Well, now, pretty lady," he drawled, showing rotted teeth. "I reckon somebody will pay a good price for you. And you'll only be a little the worse for wear."

Bridget tried to kick at him, but her feet were still bound.

He laughed, pulled a knife, and held it close to Bridget's face for a moment, no doubt expecting the gesture to subdue her into cowed silence. It didn't work, for Bridget was past caution; she had nothing to lose at this point, and she meant to go for broke.

"Leave us alone," Flossie said.

"Shut up," said the man without so much as glancing toward her. Then he proceeded to cut Bridget's bonds, freeing her feet first and then her hands. "I believe I'll just take you out into the woods a little way," he said. "Teach you how to behave like a lady."

There was a sound, only a slight cracking, but it drew Bridget's awareness like metal shavings rushing toward a magnet, and she caught the merest glint of fair hair, just out of the corner of one eye. She gave none of this away by her bearing, however, and, gathering as much spittle as her dry mouth would provide, spat into her tormenter's face.

The man drew back his arm to strike her, and Bridget was getting ready to spit again, when suddenly the camp was filled with men and horses. The "Indians," taken by surprise and still reeling from a night of revelry and thieving, fled in every direction, like chickens with a fox in their midst.

Bridget didn't take time to assess the situation; she snatched up the knife her would-be assailant had dropped and hurried to cut Flossie loose and drag her out of the fray.

She saw the paint stallion in the center of the skirmish, with Trace on its bare, glistening back, wielding the butt of a rifle like some sort of medieval weapon. He was covered in soot, from the top of his head to the soles of his boots, and his shirt was soaked through with sweat. Their eyes met, and as the other men, Jake Vigil among them, along with the marshal and Tom Barkley and a number of posse members, rode down the rest of the outlaws, he reined the paint in her direction, bent down, and lifted her up in front of him.

He looked a sight, and she was absolutely certain she'd never seen a more beautiful one.

"Fancy meeting you here, Mrs. Qualtrough," he said with a grin.

The grin told her that Skye and Noah were safe; she let her forehead rest against his shoulder for a long moment, then looked up into his eyes. "I've been a fool," she said.

He touched his mouth to hers, but only lightly. After all, they were in the middle of a crowd. "And?" he prompted.

She flushed a little. "And I love you."

"And?" he persisted.

"And—"

He waited. He wasn't going to make it easy, that was plain.

Bridget swallowed, glanced around, and lowered her eyes briefly before meeting his gaze again, steadily. "And the sooner you finish that bedroom, the sooner we can start having babies."

He kissed her again, this time on the bridge of the nose. "Oh, I don't think we need to wait quite that long," he responded, in a gruff tone meant for her ears alone.

"Skye and Noah—?"

"Skye and Noah are fine, and you know it," he said. "Unlike you, they stayed put and hid, just like I told them to."

"The house and barn?"

He sighed. "Gone. But we'll start over. There's still time enough to get some sort of shelter built before winter."

"Where will we stay in the meantime?" She hooked a finger idly between two of the buttons on his shirt.

"I reckon we'll have to sleep in that old lodge for a while, anyhow. The marshal sent them back to town for the night. His wife will see to them."

Bridget nodded, looked deep into her husband's eyes. "I've always loved you," she said.

He smiled. "I know." His arms tightened around her, and she settled close against him, a strong woman content to be held and soothed and protected. For a while, anyway.

"Trace?" She did not look up at him this time, for she felt suddenly shy.

"Yes?" His voice was low, and it echoed through her like a caress.

She kissed the hollow beneath his left ear. "Let's go home."

Epilogue

$\mathcal{B}$ridget McQuarry Qualtrough would certainly not have been the first bride to lie with her husband, beneath a blue canopy of sky and a fragrant arch of pine branches, but she might well have been the happiest. They made their bed in the tall grass, near the creek, where Trace had set up his lean-to when he first arrived, and their privacy was complete, Skye and Noah having gone to town to spend a day and a night with the marshal and his wife.

He kissed her, gently, almost reverently, and smoothed her hair back from her face with a light pass of his hand. "Bridget," he said, as though tasting her name, marveling over it, and then he grinned. He took her breath away, even covered in sweat and soot as he was. "I'm about to make love to you," he announced. "Unless you have an objection, of course."

Bridget's face heated, but she shook her head.

She might have been a virgin, she had so little experience. "I'm not sure just how——"

He laid an index finger to her lips. "Everything will be perfect," he said, and the promise sent waves of desire rolling through her, heating her blood, making her body restless. "Let me prove it."

She swallowed, then nodded.

He was fiddling with the buttons at the front of her dress, which was no cleaner than his clothes were.

She trembled. "What——?"

Trace smiled, smoothed one side of her bodice away, revealing the thin camisole beneath. Her breast strained against the fabric, reaching for him, and he smiled at that, bent his head, and touched the nipple with his tongue, leaving a wet spot on the linen.

Bridget groaned and arched her back.

"Oh, yes," Trace whispered. "Yes." Then he uncovered her breasts entirely, worked the soiled dress skillfully down over her hips. He fell to her hungrily, and she cried out in welcome, both hands cupped behind his head, pressing him close.

Trace took his time, attending to each breast in its turn, extracting whimpers and pleas from an increasingly frenzied Bridget. All the while, he was undoing the ribbons that held her now-crumpled camisole closed, and when he slid one hand down the front of her drawers to caress her private place, she nearly went mad with the want of him.

"Please, Trace," she whispered.

He kissed his way down her breastbone and made a circle around her navel with the tip of his tongue. His low groan echoed in her very bones, but he did not increase his pace. Instead, he pushed his palm through the damp nest of curls at the juncture of her thighs and began a slow, light rubbing motion.

Bridget strained against his hand, gasped when she felt his fingers slide inside her. And still it continued; he returned to her mouth, kissed her deeply, demandingly. She thought her heart would burst, it was racing so fast, and a pressure was building under Trace's palm that threatened an incomprehensibly sweet mayhem.

She had never known, never guessed. . . .

"Oh," she cried as fresh, delicious shock rocketed through her veins. *"Please—"*

He continued to kiss her, continued to ply her toward absolute madness. And then the sky split apart, and the earth trembled, and Bridget clung to Trace with both arms and sobbed while her body convulsed in ecstasy.

He brought her down slowly, as slowly as he had raised her to heaven, and when she lay still at last, dazed and breathing hard, he kissed and nibbled and teased her back to the same heated state of delicious madness she'd been in before. This time when she begged, however, he parted her legs and mounted her, and just when she thought she might claw his bare back to ribbons in her desperation, he entered her. The thrust was powerful but exquisitely controlled, as were the ones to follow, and Bridget rode back up through the clouds, careened past stars and planets, and returned to herself only when a long, timeless interval had passed.

"I love you," she said, curled against his chest, when the faculty of speech came back. "I want to spend the rest of my life with you."

He rolled onto his side, and she lay on her back in the fragrant grass, naked and free. He took a blade of that grass and teased her nipple with it, grinning. "I believe that can be arranged, Mrs. Qualtrough. And just in case I haven't said it yet, I love you, too. I think I always have."

She gave a soft moan. He was going to excite her all over again. "If you leave me, Trace Qualtrough, I swear by all that's holy, I'll come after you and bring you home."

He replaced the blade of grass with his tongue. "Don't you worry," he said. "I'm not going any-place. Ever."

She closed her eyes. Gasped with pleasure as he suckled again. "Promise?"

"Promise," he replied, at his leisure.

She smiled and, with a long, crooning sigh, gave herself up to her husband's lovemaking. One thing about Trace Qualtrough—he always kept his word.

Return to
a time of romance...

SONNET
BOOKS

Where today's

hottest romance authors

bring you vibrant

and vivid love stories

with a dash of history.

Also available from

Linda Lael Miller

The Bestselling
Springwater Seasons Series:

Springwater

·

Rachel

·

Savannah

·

Miranda

·

Jessica

·

A Springwater Christmas

POCKET BOOKS

SONNET
BOOKS

2398